Nikolai Leskov

1831–1895

A PENGUIN SINCE 1987

Nikolai Leskov

Night Owls

Translated by Hugh McLean

PENGUIN ARCHIVE

PENGUIN BOOKS

UK | USA | Canada | Ireland | Australia
India | New Zealand | South Africa

Penguin Books is part of the Penguin Random House group of companies
whose addresses can be found at global.penguinrandomhouse.com

Penguin Random House UK,
One Embassy Gardens, 8 Viaduct Gardens, London SW11 7BW

penguin.co.uk

Penguin
Random House
UK

Polunochniki first published in Russia 1891
This translation first published in the USA in *Satirical Stories of Nikolai Leskov*
by Pegasus 1969
First published in Penguin Classics 2025
001

Translation copyright © Hugh McLean, 1969

Set in 10.25/12.75pt Dante MT Std
Typeset by Jouve (UK), Milton Keynes
Printed and bound in Great Britain by Clays Ltd, Elcograf S.p.A.

The authorized representative in the EEA is Penguin Random House Ireland,
Morrison Chambers, 32 Nassau Street, Dublin D02 YH68

A CIP catalogue record for this book is available from the British Library

ISBN: 978-0-241-75219-7

The womanish babbling of the Parcae,
The trembling of the sleeping night,
The mouse-like scurrying of life.

Púshkin

I

... I had been feeling very gloomy and bored. It was still too early to leave town for the summer, but my friends had advised me to take a short excursion and see some new faces – the ones I saw every day seemed unbearably stale. Eventually I gave in to their urging and set off. I had no idea of the general lay of the land in the town where I was going and no knowledge of the customs of the people I would encounter there. Fortune, however, favored me from the very start. At the beginning of the journey I encountered some obliging and experienced persons who had taken the trip several times before, and they gave me instructions about where to stay and how to behave. I took their advice to heart and stayed where everyone stays whose calling brings him to this town. The institution in question is neither a hotel nor an inn, but a completely private house, adapted to the tastes and requirements of its guests. It is called the 'Expectension'.

I was given a small room. It was not customary for the guests to select their own quarters nor to make any complaints about their relative discomforts. This was something one learned even on the shortest visit. Everyone took the room assigned to him. Who was to be assigned to what room – this question was promptly decided by the penetrating eye of a very quick-witted woman known as the 'leash-holder'. In the absence of the 'leash-holder' herself, the sorting of visitors was performed by her housekeeper and close subordinate. Both these women were apparently of noble birth; at any rate they were ladies who had seen a good deal of the world and had formed a pretty good notion of it. The respectable age attained by both these ladies ought to have insured them against any malicious gossip, and good sense and propriety were written large on their faces, though to be sure in rather different characters. The face of the 'leash-holder' was in a dry, Byzantine style, while the housekeeper, with her arched eyebrows, belonged to the Italian school. Both these women were undoubtedly intelligent; they belonged to that species of which it is said: 'They shall not be taken in.' They smiled at each other like friends, but in their eyes there seemed to be a glimmer of other feelings quite incompatible with those of sincere friendship. A perceptive person might have concluded that it was fear of each other that bound them together.

Their extraordinary household was governed in systematic fashion. Whenever a throng or 'raffle', as they called it, of customers arrived, the ladies would meet the guests and sort them out on the spot. Those they knew were taken straight to their regular rooms, but strangers were subjected to a preliminary scrutiny, after which each expectant in the 'Expectension'* received the quarters he deserved.

As a preliminary test all the expectants were hustled into a corner to pay their respects to the icon of the Blessed Virgin. There, in nervous expectancy, they would say a brief prayer

---

* The word 'Expectension' [Russian *azhidátsiya*, a contamination of *azhitátsiya*, 'agitation' and *ozhidánie*, 'expectation'] is used here in two senses: a) as the name of the institution where people 'expect' [the favors of the religious personage domiciled in the town]; and b) as the act of 'expectation' itself. In the former case it is written with a capital letter, and in the latter with a small letter.

before the huge image, and on the basis of this they were appraised and classified.

This rather large two-story house was entirely given over to lodgings for 'expectants'. Business was evidently done simply, but on a solid foundation. Great economic, executive, and police power was concentrated in the hands of the housekeeper, but the 'leash-holder' kept the moral and political authority to herself. The domestic complement of the 'Expectension' was rounded out by a number of female servants, kept continually on the run. Besides them the house boasted a 'chefess'. All these people belonged to a rather low class of servant types. However, the 'chefess' possessed a long woolen cape, dating from her service with some 'general'. She was still very proud of it, and would wear it for her appearances before the public or 'raffle'.

There were two male employees: one stood at the door on the ground floor, while the other sat behind a small cabinet by the window at the end of the corridor. The former gave the impression of a rather dull-witted simpleton; the latter was a clever and foxy old retired soldier.

In layout the 'Expectension' was well adapted to its function as a place of expectancy. A long corridor extended the entire length of both floors, dividing them down the middle, with stalls along the sides. These were the 'rooms for expectants'. Here people were not called 'new arrivals' or 'visitors', but 'expectants'. This was felt to be more respectable and appropriate.

The corridors both upstairs and down were spacious and well-lighted, with a window at the end of each. The downstairs corridor was kept only moderately clean. It was impossible to maintain any very high standard of cleanliness, since people entered it directly from outdoors and used it as a place for

3

taking off their wraps and wiping their shoes. There was a small stove there for heating samovars and an entrance into the kitchen, from which emerged a smell of fish and mush-rooms. On one of the walls hung a large icon of the Blessed Virgin with a smaller icon alongside it; there was an icon lamp and a lectern in front of them. A well-worn prayer-rug lay on the floor, and on the opposite side stood a bench with a back, one of the so-called 'hard sofas'. In various places there were photographs and prints – all portraits of the same person in clerical garb.

On entering, all the expectants were expected to go and pray to the Mother of God, or, as they said, 'fall before Her'. Then they were all taken to their rooms.

Habitués had their favorite rooms, which seemed to be per-manently reserved for them. Some of them would even omit the ceremony of praying in the corridor and go directly to 'their' rooms after greeting the hostesses, whose only reply was 'This way, please.'

Of the others, those who were first in line and looked pre-sentable on inspection were given vacant rooms on the first or second floor. They made up the aristocracy of this strange household. Their assignment was given them promptly; they were not obliged to wait until the others had been disposed of. All the rest were taken in hand by the housekeeper and shown into the public dormitory.

The retired soldier, armed with a very severe expression, was installed behind a little yellow cabinet by one of the win-dows in the lower corridor. A boy of about nine, bearing a remarkable resemblance to the ex-soldier, sat beside him on a small stool. In front of the boy there lay a heap of opened envelopes, from which he licked off the stamps and pasted them in an album. This operation he performed briskly and skillfully, with a striking and by no means childish air of solemnity which evidently fascinated the cook, who stood beside him in her woolen cape. She watched him for a long time; at last she gave a sigh and said, 'Look at him go! His little hands scamper along like a mouse's paws!'

This diligent youngster's father evidently occupied a position of some importance. He sat solidly on a well-padded chair, under which a soft rug was spread. The ex-soldier kept glancing through some notes and making calculations on a small abacus, but this did not wholly engross him. He had eyes and ears for everything. No one could go by him without his looking up and following the passerby with his eyes and moustache.

His cabinet was covered with a soiled black oilcloth on which there were an inkstand with a quill pen and several sheets of cut paper. In the middle of the cabinet there were several unused remembrance books, oil for the icon lamps, wax candles and incense, and also a number of pamphlets and photographs of various sizes. This warrior was well along in years and undoubtedly a man of very firm character. The servants had nicknamed him 'Fishback'.

The rooms on the lower floor of the 'Expectension' were a bit on the dirty side and had a sourish smell, apparently inseparable ingredient of all the meat pies with peas import there from various places. All the 'chambers' but two had window each, with thin curtains, pricked full of holes in th middle where it was convenient to pin them. The furnitur was rather scanty, but each stall had a bed, a clothes-rack, a small table, and chairs. In the two big rooms, which had two windows apiece, there was a wretched oilcloth sofa. One of these rooms was called the 'dormitory', because it was used for those expectants who were unable or unwilling to take

5

private rooms for themselves. There were icons and portraits in all the rooms; the dormitory had a much bigger icon than the other rooms, and an 'ever-burning' lamp was kept burning before it. There was another 'ever-burning' one before the Mother of God in the corridor.

There were also lamps for the icons in the private rooms, but these were lit only when the expectants entered – and even then it was assuredly at their expense, since there was an alms cup alongside marked 'For Oil'. The lamps were lit by the warrior who maintained the trading post in front of the cabinet in the corridor.

Some of the expectants were not content with the light of the icon-lamps and in addition affixed wax candles in front of the icons in the private rooms. This practice was permitted and even encouraged, but only at times when the expectants were themselves in their rooms and were not asleep. On leaving their rooms or going to sleep they were obliged to put out the candles, but the icon lamps were allowed to burn all night.

There had been cases when people after praying and going to bed had left the lighted candles to burn out, but the 'leash-holder' or her assistant invariably noticed this and would immediately knock at the door and ask them to put out the candles. They were very careful about this, and no one was allowed to violate this rule.

The upper story of the 'Expectension' was much cleaner and nicer. The corridor was just as wide as the one below, but incomparably better lighted. It looked pleasant and even cheerful, and was used as a place for walking and conversation. In the windows at either end of the corridor were pots of the favorite flowers of the merchant class: geranium, impatiens, red burdock, and camphor wood, which was apparently powerless here against the enormous numbers of moths. In one window the flowers stood directly on the windowsill, while the other window had a cheap black wicker flower stand. Up above under the curtains there were two bird cages, one for a canary, the other for a siskin. The birds hopped about, tapped on their perches with their beaks and chirped at each other, and the siskin even sang. Here no commercial installations were in evidence. On the contrary, everything seemed designed to look respectable and proper. On the wall, in about the same place as in the lower corridor, there was another icon of the Blessed Virgin, also of great size and in a white frame with a gilded crown. It was mounted behind glass on hinges and lighted by a triple-flame lamp. On the floor in front of it there was a very clean rug with a rose pattern, and alongside stood a lectern with a cross and book on it. Both the cross and the book had a stole with a green lining draped over them.

The floor of the corridor was varnished, and shone. It had evidently been washed with soap and polished with wax. A jute runner with a flowery border stretched the entire length of the corridor.

Along the wall opposite the icon stood an armchair and several light Viennese chairs with woven cane seats. There were spittoons in the corners.

The rooms on the upper floor were much better furnished than below. Besides beds and chairs they contained dressers and washstands. Some of the rooms were divided in two by chintz draperies: one half became a bedroom and the other a sort of living room. Here there was a dressing mirror on the wardrobe and in the corner an icon, before which one could also light a lamp, or, if desired, a candle.

The candles, however, were more often used by the middling sort of 'expectants' who, properly speaking, made up the 'raffle', and lived in the lower rooms. The 'upstairs customers' usually limited themselves to the icon lamps.

Here there was no odor of pea stuffing; only inside the drawers of the wardrobes did one notice an acrid smell of Volga caviar and salmon, which had left their traces in the form of large greasy stains.

Upstairs as well as down there was a dormitory room, situated next to the 'leash-holder's' own quarters. This room, however, looked like a parlor. It was filled with overstuffed furniture and contained a large icon stand with numerous icons and in front of them a rug, a lectern with a cross and a book draped with a stole. The 'dormitory' icon lamp was kept burning, and its light was beautifully refracted in a thick glass made of crystal finely etched with diamond facets. A sealed green alms cup for voluntary contributions was affixed to the icon stand.

People slept in this room only when there were more expectants than rooms. In such cases 'extry expectants' of the same sex or a whole family were quartered there; at other times the room was considered a common meeting room and was open to all expectants who frequented the house.

After early vespers a prayer service was held there every day, at which anyone could pray and submit his requests for remembrance in the prayers of the clergy. Those who desired to arrange for private prayer services in their rooms in addition to the public ceremony had to make a special request to that effect. Such requests had to be submitted through the 'leash-holder'. The housekeeper would take no responsibility for this, and direct requests often did not reach their destination.

Candles, oil, and everything else needed for service were brought upstairs from below, and the warrior in charge of this business presented them in silence and with an air of triumphal solemnity.

General supervision of the institution was the province of the 'leash-holder' herself, who lived, as stated, in a small room on the upper corridor next to the 'meeting room'. Downstairs the housekeeper looked after things, keeping an eye on the kitchen and on the petty officer in charge of candles.

The duties of the two ladies were distinct. The 'leash-holder', as proprietress of the institution, reserved for herself the more intellectual sphere: she kept the helm of the ship. She alone knew the workings of her treasury and its devious sources of income. It was she who gave the proper tone to the whole undertaking and who had the power to obtain special spiritual consolations for those who were intelligent enough to seek her aid in procuring them.

Hers was, so to speak, the general sphere, while that of the housekeeper downstairs was more strictly confined to the narrow economic matters of transportation and petty affairs. The latter even occasionally ran into trouble, because she had to deal with the servants, who were chosen from among people of the lowest sort, and with expectants from that class of society which is called 'undistinguished'. The 'undistinguished' character of this class is expressed not only by its station in life and relative poverty, but also by its coarse habits and not infrequent lack of honesty in monetary dealings. The 'leash-holder' kept aloof from all conflicts of a pecuniary sort and had a reputation for 'kindness'; but the servants called her a 'big skinflint' and said it was 'terrible' the way she kept after the housekeeper to protect her interests and income. The housekeeper had to resort to all sorts of tricks to get the bills paid.

'All power is in their hands' – such was the general consensus.

2

I arrived there without any recommendations. I might have obtained them, but this did not enter into my modest and unambitious plans. I only wanted relief from boredom and vexation of spirit, and therefore I presented myself as an ordinary 'expectant'. As an average sort of person, I was placed under the direct supervision of the ladies in a small room upstairs.

Not knowing how I was expected to act, I watched others and tried to imitate people of experience in everything I did. This was the only way I could fall in with the prevailing tone of the institution where I was accommodated, which was essential. I did not want to be the cause of any discord in the attitudes and feelings of this unusual group of people, whose faces showed that they had come with great and far-reaching hopes and sought to obtain what they needed at any cost. I knelt and prayed with them everywhere they did and observed all their customs as closely as I could, but this procedure soon became inexpressibly tiresome and indescribably tedious. Moreover, I had the feeling that all these people were peculiarly wary and frightened of one another, and I decided that my trip had evidently been in vain, since nothing of interest could possibly occur on this visit.

I was mistaken.

In the evening I took a short walk through the town alone, and that depressed me still more. There were a great number of pot-houses and taverns, groups of soldiers, emaciated shadows of ragged tramps, and a great many women of the well-known miserable profession roaming the streets.

I should have remembered that grace prevails where sin

abounds, but I forgot that and returned dejected and thoroughly upset. I hastily drank my fill of tea in the meeting room and then went out to stand on the doorstep. I seemed to have disturbed the cook. Wearing her cape, she was talking to some personage in military uniform and kept repeating: 'Well, what do I care! What's that to me?' So as not to annoy her, I went up to my room, intending to get a good sleep before morning, get up early, and return homeward the same morning without delay.

I was so tired and bored that bed looked very good to me. The bed, by the way, was quite tolerable, but just in case, I gave it a good sprinkling of insect powder.

My intention of getting a good sleep, however, was not to be realized. At first I was afraid of bedbugs – my nomadic life had brought me into many unpleasant encounters with them in Russian inns. Then I was overcome by a desire to determine what sort of company I had fallen among, what kind of people these were – good or bad, clever or stupid, simpletons or rogues. I could not arrive at any solution nor decide what names to call them and what category to assign them to. Meanwhile I no longer felt sleepy, and instead of getting a good rest, I was threatened by a long, vexing, tiresome night of insomnia. But fortunately, hardly had everything quieted down in the halls than I heard nocturnal noises coming from both sides of my room. Evidently I had loquacious neighbors. At first I was annoyed, but then I became engrossed and began to listen in earnest.

My neighbors on the right proved to be merely disagreeable and even, apparently, not quite upright in their behavior. From their voices they seemed to be an old man and his wife. They kept moving something around and grumbling. The old man said *sh* instead of *s* and kept drinking out of a 'glash' and saying 'on-core'. They had evidently had some sort of family disturbance and had come to settle it and to threaten some-one else, but at the same time they had much to be afraid of on their own account. Actually the old woman was the more upset; she was apparently a timid sort, while the man faced things with more courage.

'Never mind, mother,' he said to the woman. 'Never mind. Don't be shy like a timid fly. That's an old shaying of ours from the Caucashush. Wait and shee what he'll give ush – he's sure to give ush shomething. The very leasht he can give ush is twenty-five rubles. For lesh than that it wouldn't be worth coming!'

'Fine, if he only does!'

'He will, he hash to. I've already fixed her and the housh-keeper too. The head one got the whole point – how much I could hurt her or help her. I'll try to find out everything, and then she'll do her besht for ush.'

'You're a lot of use to her!'

'Oh yes, mother, I am. She needs to know what ideas people come here with, and you know how I . . . I can find out what'sh inshide a man and tell her. I'll hang around with the newcomers, talk to everybody and find out all their past life. Then they'll be able to give them a surprise – they'll know everything already. I've thought it all out. They need me! Hey, gimme an on-core!'

'But how did you put it to her?'

'How? Just the way we decided. I told her we were gentry, from the Caucasian army, abandoned – a dishrespectful son – read too many fairy shtories . . . Gimme an on-core!'

'That he doesn't pray to God, did you tell her that?'

'Yesh, I told her. I told her he doesn't pray to God, doesn't want to go in the service and spends his time making boots . . . And he takes candles from the Jews after the Shabbath. I told her everything. I told her, and for that gimme an on-core and some shalmon!'

The old woman replied, 'Take your salmon, but you don't need any on-core.'

'What d'you mean I don't need one? An on-core is just what I do want.'

'No, you don't need any on-core.'

'What d'you mean! What d'you mean I don't need one? . . . I tell you, mother, pour me out a glash, a little one! I am smart, I thought it all up – now we're going to get along.'

She poured him a glass, and he drank it down and gave a loud grunt. 'Sh-h-h!' the woman warned him.

'What are you sho afraid of?'

'I'm afraid of everything.'

'Don't be shcared, there's nothing to be shcared of. Don't be afraid of anything.'

'It might get us in a mess.'

'What mesh? What for?'

'And he can ask "What for?" As if he didn't know!'

'Well, I don't.'

'But we came with somebody else's recommendation.'

'Well, what'sh wrong with that?'

'Maybe those neighbors of ours have already missed it, their recommendation.'

'Maybe they have . . .'

'Well, they might turn up here.'

'They won't do that.'

'Why not?'

'Gimme an on-core and I'll tell you why.'

'You're a drunk!'

'Hell no, I'm a smart man. Gimme an on-core.'

'Why won't they come here?'

'Pour me an on-core and I'll tell you.'

She poured him one; he drank it off and told her he had turned in a 'suspicion' the day before against some neighbors of his, from whom this couple had apparently stolen some glowing recommendation.

The old woman quieted down; evidently she thought this an apt and ingenious scheme.

A moment later she asked him whether he had consulted anyone about some invented dream of his and what had been said. The old man replied that he had and at once lowered his voice and added, 'She gave me a good leshon in how to talk about dreams.'

'Well, how should you?'

'Watch how he listens to you, and if he puts his hand on his shide, then shtop talking right away. If he puts his hands on his shides like an offisher, that means he is getting mad. Why don't you give me an on-core? I can't get to shleep without it.'

I covered my head with my pillow and lay like that for about twenty minutes. It became stuffy. I uncovered my head again and began listening. It was hard to tell whether the conversation was still going on or not; finally the old couple seemed to have gone to sleep. It was true: I could hear the breathing of two people asleep. One of them seemed to be making a great effort to pronounce the word 'on-core', while the other sent back a thin whistle, 'fire-fire'.

'Encore!'

'Fire!'

What were they doing in their sleep – hunting somebody, or even, perhaps, executing him, shooting him down?

God bless our home!

I got up quietly and, as quickly as I could, hung my coverlet over the door from behind which the sound of this enterprise had reached my ears.

The greedy tarantula and his viper, embracing on their marital couch, had passed out of my ken.

3

But just as the scene on the right quieted down, a quite different one began behind the wall on the left.

Two women were talking. The younger one called the older Márya Martýnovna; the other was named Aíchka. (Among the Moscow merchants Aíchka is used as a nickname for Raísa.) They were speaking softly and so calmly and circumstantially that I could grasp at once even how they were situated in their room and what their relationship was.

The older one, Márya Martýnovna, was speaking to the younger, Aíchka, in an insinuating, saccharine voice.

'So, my angel, I am glad you have lain down to rest by me in your little bed. This little room is outstandingly clean, and the beddie-bye is nice and soft. Snuggle tight, my little darling. You've got to have a nice good rest; otherwise it's unthinkable for you to go on. You don't need to get up for anything. I can see your azurey eyes perfectly by the light of the nice icon lamp, and whatever comes into your little head I'll notice it right away and bring it right to your little bed.'

'No, I'll get up myself and turn down the icon lamp,' answered Aíchka in a youthful voice with a Moscow drawl.

'No, no! You mustn't get up! Look, I've already shaded the lamp with a cute little book.'

'I know you. You're not young, but you're quick on your feet.'

'I can't be anything else. I've got a needle in my insides.'

'A needle in your insides?'

'The very finest, Number 11.'

'How did it get in?'

'I was doing a fast job of sewing and stuck it into my hand, and from there it went into my body. They tried to get a doctor but couldn't. They said, "It will come out by itself," but it's been going all around me for thirty years now and it doesn't come out . . . See, now the light won't hurt your azurey eyes, so I can rest easy. I'm going to sit here by your little footsies and stroke you ever so softly, and I'm going to tell you a story.'

'Don't do that, don't stroke me, I don't like it! Sit over there in the chair and tell me a story from there,' answered Aíchka.

'But I do so want to sit right here! That's what I love best of all – to be nice to a nice lady, to do what she likes, to sit at her footsies and dream with her about all sorts of things! I remember how when we were still young girls, before we were married, we used to whisper all our secrets to each other at night, and we used to play around until we went to sleep together in each other's arms.'

'Well, I don't think it's much fun for a woman to embrace and caress another woman. There's nothing to dream about in that.'

'Caresses, my angel, bring the dreams with them. That's why people who are friendly stay by themselves to dream. Of course, you can't have such a friendship with just anyone, but if a girl has a real, honest-to-goodness friend, "what happiness, what torments" she will know! It's an experience you'll never forget!'

'I can't make it out at all.'

'I'm surprised. *I* understand it very well. When I was a girl I had a bosomy friend like that – Shúra her name was.

Oh, what a cute little thing she was, and how we loved each other! Mama used to get angry and say, "Don't squander your innocent tenderness, you little fools. Save your caresses for your husbands." But we didn't want to get married, for what more could marriage bring? The only bright spot in my life was before I got married, but then they made me a victim of those two Potiphars, and that was the end of the joy in my life.'

'You mean you were married to two men? That's interesting.'

'I buried one and married the other.'

'Oh, that way! You married one after the other!'

'Well, what of it?'

'You said you were a "victim" of two men.'

'And you thought I married them both at once!'

Márya Martýnovna broke into a cracked laugh and said gaily, 'Oh, you naughty, naughty girl! You thought I had one husband for the holidays and another for the weekdays?'

'Well, that happens too.'

'It does, my dear, it does. What doesn't happen these days? But it wasn't like that with me.'

'Some of them are cheaters. A married man doesn't tell about his first wife and marries again. He gets punished for it, but nothing happens to the second woman.'

'Yes, if she pretends that she didn't know about it, then she isn't due for any especially outstanding punishment. But even so at the trial the defense lawyers will make fun of her, and the public prosecutor will cross-examine her about shameful things.'

'What harm is there in being questioned? When a woman tells things about herself, she becomes much more interesting for everyone afterwards. And anyway you can go on living with the same man they divorce you from.'

'Yes, but then you're forced to live in sin.'

'I beg your pardon, they don't perform real divorces at the altar any more, they don't remove the crowns in the church; they only read out a decree in the courtroom.'

'But then you have to register as a single person.'

'That's of no importance!'

'Yes, according to the police regulations it's all the same, but the servants have less respect for you.'

'Pay them more, and they'll give you plenty of respect.'

'But anyway, it's impossible to live just the way the law says you should.'

'But if you have money you can live as you please, and that's even better.'

'Of course, with an outstanding capital like yours – for a young widow like you, twenty-four years old, all roads are open. You can do what you please. And I'll give you some advice: don't waste time, do it.'

'Is that your advice?'

'From my whole heart. You've got to have something to remember your youth by. You suffered with your old husband for five whole years, and that's no joke.'

'Don't remind me of him!'

'Forgive me, darling, forgive me! I didn't know you were afraid to remember the dead.'

'I'm not afraid of him, but . . . I just hate to think of how he snored at night.'

'Yes, men! If they snore, they're unspeakably nasty.'

'I used to lie awake all night long, cover my head with a blanket, sit up in bed and cry. Even now if I dream of him snoring I wake right up and can't get back to sleep again.'

'Yes, a man that snores ought not to get married, all the

more so to a young girl like you with money and your out-standing beauty . . .'

'Now don't you flatter me about my beauty – I've looked at myself in the mirror . . . Of course, I'm all right, I'm no monster, but I'm on the coarse side.'

'What makes you think you're not pretty?'

'It's not that I'm not pretty; I just don't like people to fawn on me and flatter me. It's not me they want, but my money.'

'Well, my dear, I've been living with you for quite a while and you've never told me all about your money.'

'I don't have to. I'll never tell anybody anything about my money. Money is a private affair.'

'I'm not trying to pry. I was engaged to be your companion and help you with your housekeeping. That's my job, and I do what you want me to. If you want to walk in the garden, I take you there; if it's the theater, I go there with you. You wanted to come here, and I'm useful here, because I know my way around this place, but why you are so anxious to have a special prayer service held first thing tomorrow – that I don't know.'

'And you'll never find out. What I want to pray for is my own business.'

'Well, I'm not curious.'

'Naturally! And if you stay that way you'll find it easier to get along with me. You leave my dreams alone – better tell me something about yourself.'

'What, my angel?'

'Something "outstanding".'

'Oh, you naughty, how you do pick up my words!'

'I love the way you tell stories.'

'You like it?'

'That's not quite it, but . . . Well, we used to have an old man

in the house who told us stories about Gríshka Otrépyev . . .
Sometimes it was funny and sometimes sad.'

'Yes, I do have a grammatic way of speaking. Lots of people
have thought so. Nikolái Ivánovich Stépenev, the widow's
brother-in-law, who manages all their affairs, would always
ask me to stay and talk to him when he was feeling out of
sorts after a spree.'

'Didn't he have something else on his mind?'

'Nothing, my dear, except to make fun of himself and me.
"I'm a broozer," he said. "I like to hit the bottle; and you're a
bare-tailer: you like to spread gossip. Play me a sinphony at
somebody's expense.'

'How she does tell it!'

'Good?'

'What do you keep asking me for? Just tell me a grammatic
story of your life, that's all.'

'In my life, my dear, there is nothing outstanding but
sorrow.'

'Well, then, tell me the whole sinphony: where you come
from, what your family was like, and what you had to go
through for nothing. I love to hear about people suffering
for nothing.'

'I had plenty of that. Don't forget, I come from a family of
vodka distillers, and I was the goddaughter of Bernadákin,
because Papa worked in his distillery. Papa got a big salary,
but he used to say that it was terrible how much sin he had
taken on himself on that account. Later he got scared of
the Last Judgment, but he kept on drinking and finally died,
leaving us nothing. Bernadákin had godchildren galore all
around. He didn't provide for the education of all of them,
only those whose parents had rendered outstanding service.
They decided to send me to school, but I displayed a very

strange capacity: I had a very big development for absolutely all ideas, but no memory for studies at all. I could
remember and understand everything else very well, but
not studies. No matter how hard I tried to beat the stultifica-
tion table into my head, whenever they gave me a problem
with the four rules of addition – plus-ing and minus-ing or
figuring out in your head, for instance, what's the reminder
when you take five from seven – I couldn't give the slightest
answer. It was the same with Russian. I had a very good pro-
nunciation for everything, flowery-like, but somehow the
words kept coming out peculiar. And then when the bishop
asked me a question at the public examination, "Who wrote
the Revelation of St John the Divine?" – well, I didn't know.'

'I shouldn't think so!' drawled Aíchka. 'What's the use of
that?'

'It's absolutely no use – they only mix you up. And then
when I was sixteen, my little darling, I suddenly straightened
up and got very pretty. I was a big girl, but I had a miniacute
little face and a tiny beauty spot on my chin. I looked like
a Frenchy. But then the vilest thing of all happened to me.'

'Who was responsible for that?'

'It was all my relatives' doing.'

'I might have known it.'

'They caused me no end of grief. I was a Frenchy type, but
they wanted to get me off their hands as soon as they could
and marry me to a Russian. Right after that Mama started
begging for help and trying to get them to hurry up and set
aside five thousand for my dowry. Then they found me a
suitor. What a looker he was – three yards around the waist!
A real outstanding belly he had! Just imagine, he looked like
a cucumber with a bay window!'

'The devil knows what it's all about!' said Aíchka excitedly.

'Yes, my dear, it's better not to think of him,' replied Márya Martýnovna, and went on. 'I was still afraid of everything then, but nobody asked my opinion. As soon as he arrived, he made an agreement with Mama and got away with three thousand of the dowry before the wedding. And at that the money was not my family's, but belonged to the office – it was Bernadákin's. Mama knocked off two thousand for herself. "We," she said, "brought you up and fed you. Now we've got to think of your younger sister." I didn't argue with her; I didn't know where my advantage lay. Mama discussed everything with my fiancé and tried to persuade him to respect my innocence of heart and not to nag at me. But then when he didn't get the other two thousand, he did nothing else but nag. He kept griping terribly all the time and sent me out to beg for the money and wouldn't sit home with me for anything. Sometimes he didn't even come home to dinner or to bed, and my miniacute French face and my figure and my beauty spot not only didn't attract him at all, but he got so he couldn't stand me. He started making the most insulting and cutting remarks to me for the very things that ought to have pleased him.

' "What sort of pleasure is there with you?" he would say. "What am I supposed to do, roll your bones? I adore ladies with well-padded figures." '

'You just couldn't get his imagination to working,' Aíchka put in.

'It was impossible.'

'What nonsense!'

'No, it was impossible.'

'Why, then?'

'He was as cold-blooded as a real snake. It was because I was scared of him that I stuck the needle into myself. He stepped on me, and I stuck the needle into myself instead of into the cushion. And then, when I was sick, if I felt the needle pricking me and asked him to send for a doctor and have the needle pulled out of me because I felt it, he would answer in the calmest way, "What are you so impatient about? Wait a while; maybe the needle will come out of you somewhere by itself." '

Aíchka burst out laughing and asked, 'And how did it come out?'

'The way it all came out was that the needle never did come out. He found himself a well-padded lady and went on a spree. He had such luck that he kicked the bucket. Just to spite him I married a doctor's assistant right afterwards.'

'Was he any better?'

'Worse yet.'

'Don't tell me the other one was three yards around too!'

'No! Far from it! Just the opposite – this man was as thin as a rail, but a real outstanding viper. But Mama kept after me, "Go on, marry him. You look like a Frenchy," she says, "and he is close to that breed." The only French thing about him was that his name was Pomerántsev, and the doctors used to call him "Fleur d'orange". It would have been better to call him Antichrist. I even had an omen not to marry him.'

'Oh! I love omens! What was it?'

'I was just setting off from our gate to the church with him. On the front seat of the carriage there was a curly-headed servant boy sitting with the icon. We were obviously going to a wedding, but some passerby looked in at the gate and said, "Look! They're taking somebody off to be punished." '

'That's amazing! Well, how did he punish you?'

'I went through everything, my dear. First of all, he was a real sharpster and made out that he liked my miniacute face

23

and wasn't interested in my money. When he came to ask for my hand, he was dressed up fit to thrill, like a real scion of society. He had a diamond ring on his finger and paid me compliments, saying that he was a man of taste and preferred thin, supple, graceful women. Then it turned out that was all a lie, and the ring belonged to the doctor, and he didn't like me at all. I asked him, "In that case why did you lie and pretend to be in love?" And without the slightest shame he answered, "Gold is the price; with that even you can look nice." He turned out to be peeved because he had expected a lot of money from me. When he didn't get it, he too started despising me for being too thin, and he actually began to live like he wasn't my husband.'

'For that you could have complained about him to the authorities.'

'I did complain. The chief doctor called him in and said to him while I was there, "Fleur d'orange! What is this?" And he started trying to talk his way out of it. "Wait a minute, Your Excellency, this is unthinkable. She has a needle loose inside her." And he too began to make complaints. The chief doctor was quite surprised; he ordered my husband to leave the room and said to me, "What do you want me to do now? There is nothing I can do. If you have a needle inside you, then I can only advise you to pray to God that the needle may come out of you soon."'

'My, what unhappy relations you have had with men, Martýnovna!'

'Yes, Aíchka, it's true. When I was little, people were nice to me because I was miniacute and slight, but for those very things I got nothing from my husbands but coldness and insults. Especially that doctor's assistant. He wouldn't call me anything but a "humpbacked turkey", and made up all sorts of lies about me. "I can show by anatomy," he said, "that you have a stomach and then a back, and nothing else." But the Lord God is truly merciful; He soon set me free from both of them. This same Fleur d'orange started drinking and going downhill, and once he drank himself to the point of going and renting a summer place and then hanging himself in the garden. I was left with nothing and went to live with respectable folk.'

'That's hard to do.'

'It's not bad. I have a good character, and everybody likes me.'

'Now you're bragging.'

'No, it's true.'

'Well, you lived with the Stépenevs for a long time, but they finally kicked you out.'

'Excuse me, Aíchka, no one ever kicked me out from anywhere.'

'Well, they dismissed you. You can say that for the sake of politeness, but you were really kicked out.'

'I wasn't even dismissed; I left of my own accord.'

'What did you leave for? They had a good place – "outstanding", as you would say.'

'They had a very outstanding place, but for a certain reason it began going to the dogs. Besides, there was a mix-up with this place here.'

'What place?'

'Right here, where we are staying in our present state of "expectension".'

'Well, you tell me about that right now. But please sit farther away from me, in the chair. I'm afraid of that needle of yours.'

'What a suspicious person you are! But I, my dear, have

taken on quite a bit of flesh. Feel it – it's as firm as a loaf of holy bread.'

'I won't touch you; I am very suspicious. Besides, I think you had better bring me my purse with the money.'

'I've shut it up tight in the dresser.'

'No, give it here. I like to have my money under my pillow. And now tell me, why did you leave the Stépenevs'?'

4

'The stock market clash had a lot to do with it.'

'Did you really go in for playing the market?'

'I didn't, but the Stépenevs' brother-in-law did – Margaríta Mikháilovna's, that is. It isn't a big family. There's Margaríta herself, her daughter Klávdinka and her sister, Efrosínya Mikháilovna. Both of them are widows. Efrosínya is poor, but Margaríta's husband, Rodión Ivánovich, was a first-class factory owner. He was excessively strict with his workers, though. They called him "Herod", because he kept slapping fines on them. The other brother, Nikolái Ivánovich, was more easygoing with the people, but he was terrifically industriable. He was always in a terrible rush everywhere to put items on the gender. At first he built mind-layers and used to go off on terrific sprees with navy commandeers. Wherever he went there was a great hubbub and commotion, but when he came home he insisted on an absolutely impossible degree of silence. His wife was a raving beauty and very submissive. He had her so frightened that if she was sitting alone and knocked her spoon against her saucer, she would scold herself, make a threatening gesture with her finger, and say, "You fool!" But he treated her awfully anyway

and drove her into her grave. After she died he didn't want
to marry again. He sent his son Pétya away to a German
boarding school and started living with French girls and spent
all the money from his mind-layers on them. We thought it
was all over with our Nikolái Ivánovich the "broozer". But
he came out of it again. He got together with some people
and formed a company to put items on the gender; and they
organized a deal-estate bank. Once again he was carrying
around huge sums of money, and he went and spent most of
it on a Polish lady, Krutílda Silvéstrovna. Her real name was
Klotílda, but we called her Krutílda, because she never did
anything straight, but kept twisting around until she found
some way of striking home where he'd feel it the most. Then
if she wanted anything, she had only to lock herself up in the
bedroom and not let him in, and he would agree to anything
you please only to get in after her.'

'That's the way to handle them!' remarked Aíchka.

'Yes, yes; you're right. For her sake he started studying
French, but when his son finished school, he drove him out
of the house. He was touchy because Pétya had made friends
with Krutílda's niece; so he sent him off around the world
with his navy commandeers. Krutílda chased her niece out
too. She was young and miniacute, but she turned out to be
pregnant, and Lord only knows what would have come of her.
Nikolái Ivánovich didn't know what else to do for his Krutílda.
He went around with his hair curled and combed, shaven,
perfumed, and dressed up fit to thrill and went on studying
French. He used to stand in front of the mirror, slap his thighs
and sing *"Par derrière, ma garce."* Then somebody made a mess
of the accounts in their deal-estate bank. A fearful crowd of
people – raffle they were – rushed in to get their money back,
and he came home in such a state that he shouted, "Quick!

Close the scissors and bring me the gate!" And he was furious when they didn't understand him.

'We thought he had lost his mind, but he was afraid of the market clash and brought us coupons to clip. For that job of clipping he was brought to trial, but he was lucky enough to be declared an unfortunate bankrupt. Well, Krutílda, naturally, would have given him the gate, but his sister, Margaríta Mikhaílovna, took him into her service and turned over all her affairs to him. He lasted through a couple of years very well, but then he ran into the commandeers again somewhere and got so drunk and crazy that no one could calm him down. He might lay off for a week or two, but then he would start in again and come home with terrible hallucinations. He would call one sister Blanche and the other Mimíshka – he didn't realize where he thought he was. And if you asked him to behave himself a little more properly, he would snap back, "What's this? How dare you! How long ago did you graduate as a domestic-affairs lawyer? I had enough of such sinphonies in my childhood!" At such times he always quarreled with me, but then afterwards he would make up to me terribly and joke, "Marmartýn, my Marmartýn, let me give you one altýn," and then he'd start a new quarrel.'

'And why did you get into them?'

'For the sake of his sisters-in-law. They begged me to.'

'That's no reason! Do you really think you can stand in a man's way?'

'Oh, my dear, how could I help doing it, when he was always in such a state that there was no telling what he would do? Suddenly he would feel like going off somewhere, but he didn't know where himself.'

'He knew all right.'

'No, he didn't. "I'm tired," he would say, "of being in such a state. To get myself out of it I would go to the devil himself in hell." His sisters-in-law were frightened and begged me, "Talk him out of it." So I said, "No one knows the way there – stay home." "No, Marmartýn," he said, "no; you only need to catch the Antichrist's cabman, Number 666, and he knows the way to the devil."

'And suddenly he started after me: "Come on, Bare-tailer, let's sneak out of this house on the q.t. and find Number 666 and go to the devil! Why should we stay here with people any longer? Believe me, people are all rascals! I'm fed up with them!" And he kept begging me, even with tears in his eyes, till I felt sorry for him.'

'Did you really go with him?' asked Aíchka.

'What else could I do, my dear? The women begged me to, and it happened,' answered Márya Martýnovna. 'I had come to feel like one of the family, and so when his sisters would ask me, "See, this is an outstanding situation; go along with him out of town and look after him," I went. So I had to be the victim of all his stupid jokes and wisecracks. Only the last time, when there was a real first-rate scandal, he took me along by force.'

'How could he take you by force?'

'I was buying myself some boots in a shop and wasn't paying attention to anything else. The clerk was trying to cheat me, muttering, "Wait a minute . . . First class . . . Bombé style, manufactured by Miller." Then he came in, and suddenly a sinphony from his Moscow days came into his head.

' "Hello, Sister Bare-tailer," he said, "I was riding along and saw you and remembered a very important piece of business. Pick me out right now six pairs of the very best bombé boots and let's go measure them on a certain lady." "You just go to heaven!" I said, but he threatened, "Otherwise I'll turn in a suspicion on you right away." '

'How he did keep after you!'

'Oh, he was terrible. Just like a leecher or a wet leaf in the bathhouse. He wouldn't let go. How could I bring him to his senses? In the first place he was a carouser and in the second place a debachelor, and what a debachelor! As soon as he got drunk he would forget about Krutílda and feel a new urge for feminine company – and never just for any women at all. They had to be outstanding, like questriennes from the circus, for instance, or other outstanding figures of their time. But he didn't know how to treat them generously. Wherever he was he would make a terrible disconfection, order everything in sight and yell, "Come and get it! *Chaque à sa goût!*" Many of them would get offended and wouldn't want anything. They would call him a "pig", but he didn't mind. He would yell, "Look, o infusoria! Look what I can do! I am not the U-neck Skopítsyn, who cut himself off from all but his money. I live with all kinds of sinphonies!" And then he'd start off with the first of his usual sinphonies. He'd jerk the tablecloth and all the dishes onto the floor, and when they asked him to pay, he'd answer, "Go to the devil."

'I kept expecting someone to pull a knife on him.

'So I said to his sister, "You know best, but I think he ought to be cured of his shamelessness by prayer." Efrosínya was very much taken with that idea. But he wouldn't hear a word about prayers.

' "So this is the item on the gender, is it?" he said. "You think I'm a bad lot and you can pray me out of it? I know all about religious matters myself. I drank tea with Metropolitan Macarius and ate Turkish delight with the patriarch in Constantinople, and after them even the prayers of Monomákh himself couldn't satisfy me." '

'Naturally, the most outstanding sacrifices were called for at once; but the widow Margaríta Mikháilovna Stépeneva, rich as she was, couldn't get herself out of her indefinitive mood. Of course I don't know anything at all about your money . . .'

'And you don't need to know,' Aíchka broke in. 'Go on with your story, and don't try to catch me unawares.'

'Of course. I only said that by the way. I'm not curious, but it came out anyway. Margaríta Stépeneva, as I said, has a daughter, Klávdia. She is a young and beautiful girl, quite imposing. Her beauty is in the Anglican style, but she's a little cracked in the head . . . She got her education in a school for young ladies of the female sex, where she met a certain German girl. They became bosomy friends. This girl had a cousin, Dr Versteht, and it was this Versteht who did her in.'

'What did he do, seduce her?' asked Aíchka eagerly.

'No,' answered Márya Martýnovna. 'He couldn't seduce her, because she is a girl without any feelings, but he distilled a lot of senseless ideas in her.'

'What about?'

'Well, for instance about the universal poverty of mankind. He himself was such an unheard-of sexcentric that he got along on nothing. People used to call him "Doctor No-Bills". He would treat anybody, and whatever he was paid, or even if he wasn't paid at all – he didn't care. He treated everybody just the same and even preferred going to poor people. He never refused a case, and if he was given money, he would stick it in his pocket without counting it, so as not to know how much anyone had given him. Well, this sort of indifferent behavior simply captivated her and reduced her to such a state of simplemindedness that she started thinking differently about the whole way of life of human beings. She began to wish for something special, something impossible which would cause everyone no end of grief.'

'What, did she become disrespectful?'

'You couldn't make out whether she was respectful or disrespectful, but she began to like all sorts of amazing things. Her girlfriend's brother was studying at the uniworsety. When he graduated he refused to go into the government service. This disappointed everyone, but she was all in favor of it.'

'Why wouldn't he go into the service?'

'He figured it out this way. "In the service," he said, "you can be given various kinds of jobs which I wouldn't want to do. You have to waste a lot of time on trifles to please your superiors. You have to show respect to people who don't deserve it, and you are afraid that they might turn in a bad report on you. I don't want to get mixed up with anybody in any public affairs. It's better for me to serve people according to my own ideas." So he was left without any rank, and spent the whole summer and winter in a light overcoat visiting the poor, until last year he caught a cold and died, leaving his family just like that with nothing at all. Luckily, at the funeral the Germans took up a collection and fixed things for the family. Klávdinka thought this was all just fine. Right after she met him she got very secretive with all her relatives. She started spending all her time reading the Gospels. She read and read and then threw away all her nice dresses and started worrying about the poor. She would just sit there, thinking. If you asked her, "What are you thinking about all the time? What do you want?" she would answer, "I have everything. I even have too much, more than I need, but why don't other people have even the barest necessities?" You would say to her, "What's that to you? God ordained it in this way so that there would be people to serve the rich and the rich would have people to be charitable to."

She would shake her head and start thinking again and even bring herself to the point of crying.'

'For the poor?' exclaimed Aíchka.

'Yes!'

'She liked them better than the rich, did she?'

'I used to tell her the same thing. What for? If you are sorry for them, go to church and give alms at the door. There is no reason to cry out of sympathy. But she would answer, "I am not crying out of sympathy, but from vexation, because I am stupid and wicked and can't think of anything." Well, she kept on thinking, and finally she did think of something.'

Aíchka said, 'That's interesting.'

5

'She began her new life by refusing to put on any expensive dresses or gold ornaments. "What do I need them for?" she would say. "They're quite unnecessary and not at all pleasant or gay. I feel ashamed even to have such things."'

'What was she ashamed of?' asked Aíchka.

'Because she would be wearing expensive things when others didn't even have the simplest clothing.'

'But this is done on purpose, so as to distinguish one person from another.'

'Of course! How else could you tell the cat from the cook? Her mother made her a cape out of Von Gora goat wool and covered it with plush the color of sea weed. But she wouldn't put it on.'

'What was that for?'

'"It's shameful," she would say, "to live in such luxury." She liked a simple coat better. She sewed herself a black cashmere dress with white collars and cuffs and washed and ironed it herself. So she went around looking like an Englishwoman. In the summertime she wore a light chintz house dress. If her mother gave her money or silk stuffs, she would go right off and sell the silk and give away all the money – Heaven knows who to. At first her mother used to ask her in a joking way, "What are you doing, Klávdinka? – giving it all to the church for prayers?"

' "No, Mama dear," she said. "What do I want with hired prayers? That is something everyone must do for himself. I simply give it away to people who have a hard time earning as much as they need or can't pay for teaching when their children are excluded from school."

'Her mother didn't contradict her. "Well then," she said, "give it away if you want to. Let the poor pray for you." But you couldn't get her to admit that.

' "No, Mama," she said. "It's not for that at all. It's just that my poor heart can't bear it when I see how fortunate I am, and other people are living in poverty."

' "That's just why it's not good for you to go and look at all this misery. You look at it so long that you get yourself all upset."

' "I don't care about that, Mama," she said. "Even if I didn't look at them, I would still know they existed and they were suffering. So I ought to be doing something to ease their suffering."

' "Well, join a charitable society and ride about with nice ladies. I'll give you so much money that you can give away more than all the countesses and princesses."

'She didn't want that. "I know what I have to do," she said.

' "Then tell me. What is it?"

'She wouldn't answer.

' "Why are you so sad and mournful? It hurts me to look at you! Why is it?"

' "Mama, it's because I am still very wicked. I haven't yet broken myself down; I am still fighting."

' "Who are you fighting with, my angel?"

' "With myself, Mama. Don't pay any attention to me. It will be easier for me if you don't. Somehow I'll get where I want to be, but I'm not there now, and I am disgusted with myself."

'Her uncle Nikolái Ivánovich may have been a loudmouth, but he loved her. He said, "Don't keep after her. She can't act any different. This all comes from her tactical education. I know what ought to be done with her. You ought to give her a chance to have some gay sinphonies."

'He rushed off and bought her a box seat for a performance of the *Moor of Venus*. They went for her sake, even though it was Lent. Then what did she do but burst into sobs right in the theater!'

'What was that for?'

' "I told you," she said, "that I can't stand savagery and coarseness. What you think is amusing, I consider horrid and sad."

' "What is horrid? What is sad?"

' "How could it be anything else? Such a huge, black man strangles a weak woman – and for what reason?"

'Nikolái Ivánovich said, "That's something you don't understand yet. Out of jealousy even the most educated man will shed a woman's blood for love."

' "That's not true," she said. "What kind of education is that? It's stupid and bestial! It shouldn't be like that and it won't be. I don't want to see it!"

'So they left the theater. From then on there was no end to her interjections. Decent pleasures like the theater or concerts or the opera – she didn't like any of them. Instead she would bring ragamuffin street boys into her room, give them marmalade and nuts, play the piano for them, and sing them the song about how the frogs the path did run, stretch their legs and have their fun. She felt better with them, prancing and dancing. A beautiful girl like that playing leap-frog!

'When her mother saw that, she persuaded the parish priest at confession to have a talk with her. When he came with the cross at Easter time and was having a bite to eat afterwards he started arguing with Klávdinka. "It is not well, Miss. You are in error."

'She snapped right back at him, "Yes, I thank you; I thank you. You are right. I also think we live in great error, but now I am a little happier."

' "How is that?"

' "Because I am dissatisfied with myself. I am not what I want to be. I condemn myself, for I see the light."

' "Aren't you taking a good deal on yourself?" he said.

' "I don't know," she answered, stammering confusedly.

' "That's just it!" said the priest. "But we know that in this world there must be both rich and poor. It is so everywhere."

' "Unfortunately, that is true," she replied.

' "So it is useless to talk nonsense like that, demanding that everyone be equal."

'She turned cold, and rubbing her temples, said in a whisper, "People talk nonsense without meaning to."

'And the priest said, "Yes, without meaning to. But for raving like that, even if they don't mean anything by it, they can sometimes be sent far, far away. Do not go against religion."

' "I am not; I love religion."

' "Then why do you desire the opposite?"

' "Is the desire for simplicity of life and the elimination of grinding poverty really against religion?"

' "What do you think? Did Christ acknowledge the poor, or not?"

' "He did."

' "Well then, do you seek to oppose Him?"

' "I am answering you, not Christ. Christ Himself lived like a beggar, but we do not all live as He lived."

'The priest got up and said, "So that's the way you are!" He turned to her mother and said, "Margaríta Mikháilovna! I will tell you frankly, respecting you as a good parishioner, that I have talked to your learned daughter. However, out of respect for myself I must say, madam, that it is not worthwhile talking to her. You have only one recourse: pray that she may not perish utterly."

'Margaríta Mikháilovna, all flushed and in tears, made excuses and begged his forgiveness for the mockery he had been exposed to. The priest was mollified and answered, "As far as I am concerned, of course, may God be with her. Let her babble whatever she pleases. These stupid dreams are wide-spread in society now, and we have heard our share of them. But mark my words: this evil is new, but it is as bad as the old evil of annihilism. Your daughter is treading a wicked path, wicked, wicked!"

'Margaríta Mikháilovna gave him a ten-ruble note as quick as she could, but he was not to be bought over; he pressed the money under his thumb, but went on threatening her with his forefinger and repeating "A wicked, wicked path!"

'Margaríta Mikháilovna got angry herself, and after he had gone shouted after him, "What a sour one you've turned into!"

'Yet Klávdinka kept her temper, remarking, "It is your own

fault, Mama dear. Why do you bother them? He said what he had to say."

' "Then who can help me deal with you, what powers can I call on?"

' "But really, Mama darling, why should you ask for help against me? How have I been disobedient to you?"

' "You have been disobedient in a great many ways, the most important ones. It is true, you don't answer me roughly. But you don't dress as befits a girl in our financial position, to show people what we are worth. You don't live – you trail around with beggars. You are ashamed of the wealth your grandfather earned and for which your father committed so many sins and injustices."

'At that Klávdinka seized her mother by the arm with one hand, and with the other covered her own prophetic eyes and suddenly shrieked like a theatrical actress in a quavering voice, "Mama darling! Mama! Dearest! Don't say that, don't! Let's not say anything about Father. It's too terrible to remember!"

' "No one denies – may the kingdom of heaven be his – that he was a viper. But I am the one who spoiled you, and I thought that your spiritual father, at any rate, might be able to teach you a lesson."

' "Mama! It is you who can teach me better than anyone else."

' "No, I can't, and I won't try to!"

' "Why?"

' "I am sorry for you!"

' "There, I have been taught a lesson. You took pity on me, and by that you taught me! I love you, Mama, and I will not do anything that might grieve a Christian mother. And you are a Christian, aren't you, Mother?"

'And she looked into her eyes and played up to her, and

so they made it up. Things went along quietly that way to the point where she could do anything she wanted with her mother. She not only refused to see a performance of the *Moor*; she also declined to hear the opera *The Huge Knots*. "I don't want to, Mama," she said. "Songs are good when people sing them out of feelings of sadness or joy, but to do it like that, for money, is nonsense. It's a shame to pay money to see such skeptacles. Let's give it to the poor children instead." Her mother agreed with her right off and smiled, "Well, give it to them. You must be an angel of God." The girl answered her in raptures, "Oh, if it were only true! If only I were really an angel of God!" And then she began laughing and joking again, singing and dancing. "I am so glad," she said, "I'll put on a free performance for you." And her mother was too happy for words. So it turned out that Klávdinka could do anything she wanted without even asking her mother's permission.

' "I believe," she would say, "that she loves me and would never do anything to grieve me." '

'Klávdinka began going to artificial classes where various educational fads for both sexes are allowed, and she went and joined a class for modeling ugly faces out of clay and learned how to do that. She would take and model any appurtenance you can think of. Then she learned to paint on porcelain and filled the whole house with rubbish; you couldn't even get into her room. She wouldn't let you anyway; she didn't even let the servants in. She would mix a lot of green clay in a basin, pour it out on a board like dough, and then start working it with her fingers.'

'That must have been hard,' observed Aíchka.

'There's nothing hard about it,' answered Márya Martýnovna impatiently.

'You mark off the nose and the mouth and then all the

other appurtenances – and it's all done. She could draw on porcelain, but she still couldn't get along without the Russian peasant. She had to give it out to a peasant to have it baked. Then she took all these articles to the stores to sell them. Her mother and aunt were naturally horrified. As if she were in such need that she had to sell her handiwork! All the money they had, and such consequences! But if she was given money, she would take it off heaven knows where and give it to heaven knows who. And that was just the time, you know, when both the Arrestigating Commission and a political conspuriousy were operating at the same time. Who was she taking the money to? If it was to the poor, then why shouldn't I, a poor woman who had lived with them so many years and received presents from both her mother and her aunt, why shouldn't I get a penny from her? Once I asked her myself, straight out, "Klávdinka, why don't you give me any of your righteous works? For a joke you might at least have bought me a piece of chintz with empty patters on a background of nothing." She couldn't even take a joke, but cut me off firmly, "You don't need anything; you manage to worm things out of everybody." Lord have mercy! Lord have mercy! What a heartless girl! I'm not proud, it's true. If I need something, I ask for it. But what business is that of hers? And she talked to her mother the same way. Just imagine, on her mother's name-day she picked a rose and brought it to her. "Mama, my darling," she said, "you have no need of anything." And imagine this: her mother agreed with her. "I have everything," she said. "All I need is your happiness." And she gave her a kiss for the rose. But Klávdinka went on, "Mama dear! what is happiness? I live with you and I am happy, but there are a great many unhappy people in the world."

'So she kept harping on her old idea, even on her mother's

name-day! I couldn't stand any more and I said, "Look, Klávdinka, on the name-day of your mother's guardian angel you might at least keep quiet about your gloomy ideas. There's nothing outstandingly pleasant in them at all."

'But just imagine, her mother stood up for her and told me, "Let her alone, Márya Martýnovna, and tell the servants to take the samovar away." And when I had gone out, she presented Klávdinka with five hundred rubles. "Give it to those poor wretches of yours," she said. "Lord, it is fearful to think what sort of people they are."'

'But how could you see that?' asked Aíchka.

'I just looked through a crack. But Klávdinka didn't share any of this money with anybody in the house this time either.'

'Why not?'

'Because she said, "Everyone has enough to eat here."'

'Well, she was right about that.'

'How can you say that, my dear? You ought to be ashamed of yourself!'

'Not the least bit.'

'No, you are teasing me. I know . . . As if all a person needs is to have enough to eat! And then no matter how many times I told her, "All right, now, if you are only kind to people outside your own house, why are you so anxious that no one should know who you are helping out?" She would answer, "The good man is he who cannot rest when others are not at peace. But I am not good. You do not have a proper notion of goodness."

' "All right then, I don't know anything about goodness, but I do understand secretiveness. Why do you take such pains to hide where you take everything and who you give it to? No one can track you down. Is this really admissible or required by the rules of honor?"

' "Imagine," she answered me with a smile. "Yes, it is admissible and required by the rules of honor!"

' "Then kindly enlighten me, madam," I said. "Show me where these rules are, what holy book they are written in."

'She went into her room and came back with a small volume of the Gospels.'

'Always the Gospels!' interrupted Aíchka.

'Yes, yes! All the time! She was always reaching for her Gospel and dragging out some text I had never heard of in my life. Besides, she didn't understand them properly. She would always think up some quite simple and ordinary explanation that was not even interesting. Then she would give me the Gospel and say, "Here's something you can do for yourself. Read this passage." And she showed me the passage about how my right hand shouldn't know what my left hand is doing and that you shouldn't do favors just for your own circle of friends who can repay them . . . And so on.

'I knew I couldn't get the better of her in an argument, so I answered, "The Gospel is a Church book, and its wisdom is sealed. Not everyone can understand it."

'She objected right away, "No, that's just the point: the Gospel can be understood by anyone."

' "Well anyway," I said, "I had better leave the Gospel alone and ask the priest. Whatever he tells me I'll agree with, because they are the clergy."

'And so I really did get the idea of arguing her out of it, and I went to the parish priest. The year before I had made him a present of a rose geranium plant. His mother was bothered by running wax in the ear, and the geranium leaf is a good cure for it: you just stick it in your ear. This time I went to the market and bought a titmouse. I took it out of its cage and tied it up in a handkerchief and brought it to him. He didn't like people to come to him without an offering.

'Once he had complained to me that there were an awful lot of bedbugs in his house and that they couldn't get rid of them. So I said, "Father, here is a titmouse for you. It both sings and exterminates bedbugs. Only please don't feed it anything – out of hunger it will go all over the house and pick the bugs out of every crack and cranny." '

'Is that really true?' asked Aíchka.

'What?'

'The titmouse, does it really pick out bedbugs?'

'Of course! It gets them all!'

'Amazing!'

'What do you mean? It's the most ordinary thing in the world. All our distillers and priests used to keep titmice for that. Anyway, the priest thanked me. "I know it," he said. " 'Tis an ancient remedy. Put the titmouse back in its cage. When it has gotten its bearings, I'll let it fly around the room and catch bugs. The insect powder they sell nowadays is worthless; it has no effect at all. It's all adulterated."

'I caught him up on that last remark, saying that it was impossible to tell what anything was like any more. And I told him about Klávdinka's antics with the Gospel. "Is there really a law in the Gospel," I asked, "that says we should give up our acquaintance with important people and mingle only with the poor?"

'He answered, "Hearken, O oaken grove, to what the forest saith: these people interfere in what is not their affair. They can pick out texts, but they know not how to interpret them, and what they educe is vain and false."

' "And why," I inquired, "haven't you informed the authorities about these false texts of theirs?"

' "We have," he replied. "We have, many times."

' "Then how can they dare to judge for themselves and base their ideas on the Gospel?"

' "That is the way things are. The mistake is already made. These books have been printed in large quantities and sold to all and sundry for practically nothing."

' "And why is that?"

' "Well, it's a long story. People used to complain that the Scriptures were badly taught. Even then I used to say, 'They are taught well – as much as each man needs. Cast not pearls before swine; they will trample them under their feet.' And that is just what they are doing now – trampling them in the mire. And so this was the result: in the fields, failure of harvest, and among men, that incomprehensible disease called Bethluenza."

'So, to make a long story short, he spoke very well, but didn't give us any help. He even came to see them later, but when he was saying good-bye to her all he said was, "You are oversalting it, Miss, you are oversalting it!" But soon after that she went him one better: she went off and disappeared altogether.'

'Did she really disappear completely?' asked Aíchka.

'No, she sent her mother a dispatch, saying that a poor girl friend of hers had come down with the black smallpox; her mother was too old to do anything and nobody would look after her. Dr Versteht had undertaken to treat her. Our Klávdinka had dropped in to see her and stayed on as a nurse, sending home this dispatch and asking her mother's pardon for not coming home – she was afraid of spreading the infection.'

Aíchka sighed and said, 'Believe me, she really had gone to the dogs!'

'Yes, maybe so; but if you talked to her, she still pretended that this too was according to the Gospel. She didn't care a fig for all the agonies her mother suffered, wondering whether she would come home pockmarked or blind. When she did come back – safe and sound – they had the priest talk to her again. And again he told her, "You are oversalting it terribly!"

'But she had a joke ready for him. "It's better that way, for if the salt shall lose his savor, wherewith shall it be salted? That's worse still."

'But the priest caught her nicely on that one. "It is not enough, Miss," he said, "to know texts. You must know more. The salt that loses its savor is not the salt that everyone uses now, but a weak Palestinian salt. Our salt is strong; it does not lose its savor. And so we have our own proverb about salt: 'Undersalted – on the table; oversalted – on the back.' It would do you good to know that. In other words, you can add salt to something that is undersalted, but for oversalting you are whipped."

'But it didn't matter what you said to her; she wasn't afraid of anything.

'Then I said to her mother, "It's obvious that no ordinary priest can put the fear of God in her. She needs something outstanding." And I told her about the man from here.

'Her sister Efrosínya was simply bowled over with joy and started telling stories about things that had happened here.

' "Let's try it," I said. "We'll apply to him, and invite him here. Incidentally, it would also be a good thing for Nikolái Ivánovich, for his abstinence."

'But Margaríta Mikháilovna looked somehow embarrassed. I saw that she was hiding something when she answered, incorrectly, "In my sorrow no one can be of any help with her."

' "Why not?"

' "Because she still orders her life according to the Gospels."

' "Please, enough of that," I said. "You have despair in your heart, and despair is a mortal sin. It would be another matter if

45

it was the money you were worried about; he has no definite arrangement about how much you should give him. But whatever you give him, he doesn't keep anything at all for himself, not the least bit, but spends it all on good works. And Klávdia Rodiónovna herself worships good works."

' "It isn't the money I care about," she said, "but . . ."

' "The trouble – is that it?"

' "Not the trouble either. But what sort of faith will he find in us? That's what disturbs me. And it is not only Klávdinka. My brother-in-law Nikolái Ivánovich – he became an elder of the Church only for the sake of the decoration, and he certainly won't want to pray for his own abstinence."

' "Of course, my dear; but there is a remedy for that. We won't tell him that we are praying for him; we will pretend it's for Klávdinka."

' "And Klávdinka will be still more offended."

' "Well, we'll conceal it from her too: we'll tell her it is for her uncle."

' "And so we will start off by deceiving everybody. Is that a proper way to behave?"

' "What's that? Yes, of course there will be a little deceit at the beginning, but they will profit by it in the end."

'Margaríta was about to give in; I struck while the iron was hot and offered to go myself and arrange everything here. "I'll find some outstanding people who know everything," I said, "and I'll go there and invite him, and then go meet him in a carriage. All you'll have to do is to give me the expense money."

'She replied, "That's not the point. But if he really does see right through into people's insides, I'm afraid of him, and I'm surprised you're not scared too. Or are you both free from sin?"

'Her sister Efrosínya Mikháilovna and I assured her that we were not free from sin, but that she didn't have to be afraid, because even if he could see right through you, he kept everything he saw to himself and didn't announce it to the world. Finally I asked her, "What particular sins do you have on your conscience?"

' "I have some," she said.

' "But what sort of sins are they?"

' "Well," she said, "I don't really know myself. But whenever I start something against Klávdia, it comes out badly."

' "Well, that is temptation. And what else?"

' "Besides that, my brother-in-law Nikolái Ivánovich has been living with Krutílda out of wedlock, and to please her he drove his own son Pétya out of the house. I am afraid of embarrassing him."

' "My dear lady," I said, "he did that to please a woman! Men in love always behave nastily to their children. These are all completely unoutstanding trifles!"

' "No," she said, "it's no trifle to drive your own child out of the house. I have been on tender hooks for a long time, waiting for Klávdinka to make a violent scene with her uncle because of his injustice to Pétya."

'I realized that she was just twisting about in her mind. What she was really afraid of was that he would discover something inside her beloved Klávdinka. But this time I didn't stand my ground; the hour for fulfilling the will of God had not yet struck.

'Once again she undertook to give Klávdia some diversion; she tried to get her to take seats for *The Huge Knots* and to hear Barebald, but she lost patience with her and said to me, "Dear friend, Márya Martýnovna. We consider you one of the family, and we always come to you for help eventually. Would you go out after her and see where she goes and who she gives her money to and why she doesn't want any pleasure in life?"

' "Certainly, for you I'll do it," I said.

'After that as soon as Klávdinka left the courtyard, I was after her like a police defective, but I kept my distance. If she walked, I walked; if she took the streetcar, I sat in the next car; if she took a cab, I did the same. I never let her out of my sight. Once, twice, three times I chased after her like that, and finally I tracked her down. The place she went to most often was a small white house, where she darted into one of the apartments with her packages. I went right to the janitor, gave him a tip and started questioning him. "Who lives in that apartment?" "A poor old woman occupies it," he said. "Who comes to see her?" "A young girl and the woman's nephew." "Is the nephew young?" I asked. "He certainly is!" "And do they meet there?" "Sometimes they come separately, sometimes together."

'I had caught my little bird!'

'You may have caught her, but don't press on me. I told you, you may be as round as a loaf of holy bread, but I am still afraid of your needle,' Aíchka interposed in a prolonged and sleepy drawl.

'Oh, you cute little thing! At least let me kiss your sugary little shoulder . . .'

'Not for anything in the world! My shoulders were not made for such kisses. Go on with your story.'

6

'I went back home to the Stépenevs and told them everything as best I could.'

'Well! I'm sure you did a good job of that!'

'Of course I did. A young fellow meets such an outstanding girl at an old woman's flat – do you need to guess what they do there? By the way, don't think I told her mother that. I only told her aunt, Efrosínya Mikháilovna. She recalled that their mother had been an Old Believer, and although she was extremely respectable in her behavior, she was still listed as a "spinster" in her porter's records. So she was sorry for Klávdia and gave me thirty rubles, saying "Keep still about it, my dear Martýnovna. Don't tell anyone about this grandezvous, for that which is done in secret shall be judged in secret. If it has already happened, let her have her fun. She has a miniacute figure and *it* won't be noticeable; meanwhile we'll find her a husband. Then she won't be so capricious any more."

'Aunt Efrosínya Mikháilovna started going to see matchmakers, trying to find a husband for Klávdinka, and she had considerable – you might even say outstanding – success. But just imagine, no matter who came and asked to marry her, she always gave the same answer: "I don't know his way of thinking; it is essential for us to be of the same mind."

'That's the way they do things – they don't choose a man for his family or his money, as they should, or like him for the exterior of his person. They choose people for their thoughts!

'Then she suddenly announced that she was of the same mind as a doctor relative of Versteht's. When her mother Margaríta, who is quite a portly woman, heard that, she plumped right down and sat on the floor. Klávdinka was about to help her up, but she ordered her, "Let me alone. Kill me right here! Is he a German?"

' "Yes, Mother."

' "And what is his faith?"

' "He is a Reformist."

' "What do you mean, 'Reformist'? What sort of a thing is that for us to be related to?"

'Uncle Nikolái Ivánovich was a little tipsy and said, "I know what Reformists are. They're the people they hang."

' "Lord!" And Klávdinka half turned toward him and said, "Uncle, stop getting Mother alarmed and making a fool of yourself. There is a Reformist Church."

'Nikolái Ivánovich said, "That's another matter, but the item on the gender is that I, as the outstanding member of this household and a loyal putriot, desire you to marry an upright man of the true Orthodox faith."

'She answered, "What are you talking about, Uncle! When did you turn into a theologian? You talk like that, but you haven't the slightest idea what Orthodoxy is."

' "No, now you are lying! I was an elder and I even wangled a belly-band for my priest."

'At that Klávdinka gave him a gentle pat and said, "That's all you do know, how to wangle belly-bands. You had better get up off that stool and have them clean you off. You are all smeared with clay."

'Nikolái Ivánovich went out, and that ended it. But the next day he went in to see her again, drunk as a lord and seeing pink elephants with goats' feet all around. Again he said to her, "Who would have expected a nice girl, the heiress of a merchant family, to mold such a monstrosity as this? What are these dummies for?"

'She wasn't at all angry and said, "Order something else of me, and I will make you whatever you order."

'Her uncle said, "All right. I would like to order a statue from you, but it must be a religious one."

' "What shall it be?"

' "Make me my patron saint Nicholas, showing how he slapped Arius in the face. I'll take it and pay for it."

' "It would be better to show him caring for the poor or saving the condemned youths from execution."

' "No, I don't want that. I give to the poor myself, and I have seen people executed . . . That too is absolutely necessary . . . A priest accompanies them to the scaffold . . . But you show me how the saint smacked Arius on the cheek in the midst of the Council."

'So a new argument broke out between them – about executions, and about the slap. At last Klávdinka said, "I can't do that."

' "Why not? What do you care?"

' "In the first place, I do care, because it is good to work on things you like, and I don't like that. And in the second place, thank God, it is now known that that fight never took place at all."

'Nikolái Ivánovich was surprised at first, but then he started shouting, "Don't you dare to say that to me! Because it did, yes, it did! He smacked him right in front of everybody!"

'Klávdia said, "No, he didn't!"

'Her uncle said, "You are only arguing with me to annoy me, because I revere him."

'Klávdia answered, "But it seems to me that I revere him more than you do, and I want you to know what you ought to revere him for."

'To settle the argument Nikolái Ivánovich decided to go to midnight mass and after that to go see some professor and ask him whether the affair with Arius really happened. So he went off, and the next day he said, "Imagine, yesterday I was playing pilliards with the professor. I took up the item on the gender with him about Arius, and he actually confirmed what our learned girl here said – the saint wasn't present at that Council after all. I was very sorry to hear it. I am likely to go through a terrible religious upheaval, because I liked that incident best of all. I flew into such a rage yesterday that I even let loose a pilliard ball at the professor's forehead. Now he is going to bring charges against me, and I will either have to suffer imprisonment for my faith, or else I will have to go and beg his pardon. That's the sort of calamity that Klávdia has brought on me!"

'He sat down and burst into tears. At that Efrosínya Mikháilovna stood up for him and said to her sister, "You know best, Margarítenka, but what is this really, when everyone is crying on account of Klavdyúsha? Now even I feel frightened in your house; I'd like to run away."

'Then Margaríta broke down and turned to me, "Please, Martýnovna, go and invite *him* here."

' "It's high time," I replied. "This is now such an outstanding situation that all the ingredients can be mixed up in such a way that no one will be able to make out who we are doing it for. Nikolái Ivánovich will think it is for Klávdinka, and Klávdinka will think it is for Nikolái Ivánovich."

'Both Margaríta and Efrosínya covered me with kisses.

' "You are the clever one," they said. "Go off, darling, and do everything right and proper, so I won't have anything to do but pay out money."

' "All right, but write me a letter of introduction in your own name and in that of Nikolái Ivánovich, as the outstanding member of the family, so that I'll have something to invite him with. Without that it is unthinkable."

'They agreed. The only difficulty was who would write the letter. The old women both wrote like hens scratching and were ashamed of their penmanship, and as for me, my n's and u's always look just alike, and sometimes you can't make any sense of it. Besides, we didn't know how to subscribe it: simply "To His Excellency" or "To His Super-Excellency"?

'We thought of appealing to Klávdinka; she had studied the catechism more than anyone else and ought to know all the forms for addressing the clergy. But when we asked her to come out of her room and write a letter for us, we had trouble with her again. She came out, sat down, and picked up the pen, but when she found out who we were writing to, she put it down again, wiped her hand, and stood up.

'Her mother asked her what she meant by that, and she apologized, "Mama, I don't know how you ought to write to these gentlemen. Besides, if you will allow me to give you my opinion, I wonder why you summon a person from so far away when there are others of that calling nearby. Since they all do exactly the same thing, why offend your neighbors?"

'The old woman thought that over. I realized that a case of this singular aspect would lead to an infinitive discussion, so I broke in. "Let it go," I said, "I will zip down to the fur shop on the Avenue. There are always people in expectension there, and they must know how to write him letters." So off I zipped.

'They wrote it for me right away, and I went off to see Nikolái Ivánovich and have him sign it.'

'You are a busybody,' drawled Aíchka.

'Yes, I have a needle inside me . . . I have always been pert and lively like that. But just imagine . . . Tell me, do you believe in temptations, or don't you?'

'Well, sometimes I do and sometimes I don't.'

'You believe in them once and for all. I have always believed in them, and they always come as though on purpose just when a person is drawing close to faith. So just imagine what happened . . . !

'I didn't find Nikolái Ivánovich in their store. The clerks

said he was on a spree again and had gone off with some dry-goods Dutchman to the "Pagánistan" to have lunch and knock balls around. I went into the "Pagánistan" and sent the porter up with the letter for Nikolái Ivánovich to sign. But he had already chased out all the Dutchmen and was sitting alone, drinking black coffee with cognac in it, and he asked me to come into his private room. I went in and saw that his face was the color of Burbondy. He still hadn't cooled off from the night before, and he added plenty of new zest to the old yeast. He tried to read the letter, but he couldn't make anything of it. He kept the paper in his hand and asked me, "Why has this epistle to the Corindians been composed? I can't make it out at all."

' "That was what you wanted," I said. "To perform an outstanding act of piety and to give Klávdinka a useful bit of edifyance."

' "But now I don't care any more," he said. "If Arius didn't get a smack on the face, then no one needs any edifyance."

' "But we have already made a political conspuriousy," I said, "to take this learned girl of ours, turn her upside down, and give her a smack that will redden her cheeks. So look here! This is the person I want to bring to see her; all you have to do is sign this letter and go to meet him when he comes. It won't be hard for you to put on all your appurtenances for just an hour."

' "No," he said, "the way the item on the gender is now, I am upset to an outstanding degree. The most harmful sort of consequential affairs are being uncovered in my deal-estate bank, and if people find out on top of that that I am calling in some special Reverence, they are certain to think I am completely cleaned out, and that would be the worst thing that could happen to me. I don't want to have anything to do with your female political conspuriousy."

'I saw what a regardless state he was in and asked him to come home with me, but he wouldn't hear of it.

' "How long is it," he said, "since you passed the exams for domestic affairs lawyers? I'll either give you a good domestic beating right here and now, or else I'll put an item on the gender and call in a political defective from the public room there and turn you in to be questioned for your conspuriousy. But if you want to escape all that, come along with me, we're going to a lying-in home."

' "Why a lying-in home of all places?"

' "We're going there to pick up a certain staff midwife by the name of Márya Amourovna."

' "What has happened, have you gone completely to the devil? What do I want with a staff midwife?"

'But he was so indesistant that he stuck to me like a leecher or a leaf in the bathhouse. He had this midwife on the brain and started praising her to the skies, so high I couldn't even make out just what her situation was.

' "Márya Amourovna," he said, "calls herself a midwife only for the appurtenances of the title, but she lives as she pleases. We'll go to the Hotel Angleterry with her and we'll have a drink of Cluquot with her, *en trois*, in a nice and proper way. Then she will do a dance by herself."

' "Then why go *en trois*?" I said. "I don't want to. You two go off by yourselves."

' "No," he said, "now there is a persecution of members of the female sex who take rides alone with men. Márya Amourovna might get in trouble. You'll be a sort of lady relative for us; we'll keep you behind a screen. For that I'll give you a cape made of caramel hair."

'He kept after me until I gave in. We rode and rode *en trois*, and he kept hanging on to me like a leecher. I had to go with them and see all his infamies. They dilly-dallied there till morning, and I slept behind the screen. Finally the midwife started quarreling with him louder than before, and he fought back, and she went off alone. Then I managed to persuade him to come out and get into the carriage. But all the way he kept trying to go back, saying "It's still early for me; I am a night owl."

' "What do you mean – night?" I said. "Look at the clock on the watchtower: it's already morning!"

' "That clock doesn't show its hand properly," he replied. "I can tell because I smell hic-scents; that means that the fuddle-drummers and saloon-players are still riding around in their night cabs. So it's still long before morning."

'Then suddenly he got the notion that he had been given someone else's hat in the "Angleterry". I couldn't convince him that he had his own hat on his head, which he did.

' "No," he said, "I remember very well. I had on a round bowler; then why should I have a flat topper on now? Maybe this is part of your political conspuriousy – they'll take a mon-umentary picture of me like this, and then I'll have to answer for you or some other dame and I'll be sent off to places so far away that the angels themselves don't know where they are . . . No, you won't catch me in any conspuriousy. I'll show you what a political trial is, and I'll shout, 'Save, O Lord . . . ' "

'And he started to call a policeman. To calm him down I said, "The devil take you anyway! Go back to the 'Angleterry'; I agree to all your prepositions."

'He quieted down. "Good," he said. "That's what I like to hear. Now we won't go back there; you and I are going to a dancing party. People criticize the hosts because honest women don't come to their parties; well, instead of an honest woman I'm bringing you. We can go on with the party there till late in the morning . . . But listen! Keep mum about this at home! Not a word!"

‘ "Of course," I said. "Mum's the word. Why should I want to tell people about my shame and the places you have dragged poor little me into?"

‘He started making up to me and said, "If you want to be easy in your mind, don't get bad ideas. This is a public place; there are no crooks here – only people of various sorts, like Popular Councilors and machinators. When we are together here we see each other's uncognitos and call each other 'pal'. There are three musket ears: Tupas, Tushas, and Tulas, and I am their commander. Tupas is a merry Dutchman; Tushas is believed to be a chemist in a factory, but he isn't that at all – he's really a great attorney-at-law; he'll turn you inside out – and Tulas is a machinator and ties everybody in knots. All you have to do is show him someone's card and he'll do the rest – make friends with him, tie him up, and deliver him into your hands."

‘ "Lord! What is that for?"

‘ "For whatever you want or don't want," he replied.

‘ "Do you get a big salary?"

‘ "The defective and the machinator do," he said. "But I entered this combination out of a noble desire for respectability, and now I can't get out of it."

‘The members of this gathering turned out to be mostly cocotties of all sizes. The big ones had on a random assortment of negligees, and the little ones were in silk undies, some of them in modest black ones, as if they were in mourning. They all went up to Nikolái Ivánovich like old friends and shouted "Commander!" "Commander!" I didn't embarrass them in the least; they shook hands and asked me politely, "Met tay voo plass," which means "Take a seat." But imagine this: as soon as he saw the defective and the machinator, he got that political conspuriousy on the brain again and whispered in my ear, "You, if you please, will drink and not refuse anything, because this machinator is whirling before my eyes right now, and if I should get mad at you, I might tell him about the conspuriousy, and after that he might even mix me up in it."

'I was more dead than alive. I thought I might let the cat out of the bag if I got drunk, but I was forced to drink anyway, and I didn't know how it would all end. The company was as awful as could be: this Dutchman looked like a watermelon from Komýshensk; the defective and the machinator were both small, but had terrific moustaches. There still weren't enough people for Nikolái Ivánovich, and he kept calling in people at random and introducing them to me. "This man is an actor," he would say, "and I am very fond of him. He has grown old amusing people around the dinner table." Then he would kiss him and say, "Have a drink, old man! This man is a scribbler; he will write me a tender epitaph for my name-day. This one is an artist; he is going to draw me a plan for the statutory in the garden of Krutílda's summer place. This one is a basso rotundo in the opera; he sings better than Petróv." Then he would drop all the men for a while and try talking French to the cocotties in mourning. But he wasn't good at it; he kept putting in "Come-on dear, come-on dear", and they answered, "tray share tea" and "tray John tea". He kept gurgling tur-tur-tur and "pear met tay mwa sore tear" and stammering and jerking back. Then in Russian he would order something brought right away; they had to bring him everything – things they wanted and things nobody wanted. The Frenchies said nothing but "passay" and "passay back", but they only pecked at the food, they didn't eat. The waiters kept bringing in more and taking away the stuff they had pecked at. Behind the buffet they kept adding everything in triple strength to the bill, but he went on ordering, "Cluquot, Cornichons, Bradelaise, this kind of cigars and that kind!" They kept up their "passay" and "passay back" and finally got tired of eating. Then they only drank and clinked glasses and got into an argument about actors.

'The actor started counterdicting the basso rotundo and telling him he could never stand up to Petróv. They went on cursifying each other so awfully that all the cocotties left. The musket ears kept on slinging mud at each other at random and saying that nothing was any good. Someone even shouted that even Petróv was not worth talking about. The other would shout back, "I like Timberlick best of all." Someone else said, "I hear Calzonari and Bosio" . . . "And I remember Barebald's appearance in *Il Drove Adore* and Lavróvskaya's in *The Magic Marcher*." Then someone said of Lavróvskaya, "Why does she wink her eyes when she sings?" Nikolái Ivánovich stood up for her and shouted out that he admired Lavróvskaya most of all. He tried to imitate her, winking his eyes and singing in falsetto,

> *The bronze horse fell in the field*
> *And I ran up afoot!*

'One of the military men didn't like this and said, "Instead I'll sing you our regimental song from the Caucasus" and came out with:

> *Neath the Corkissus's crags*
> *With a shot in my insides*
> *I joyfully dropped off to sleep.*

'The others divided up and took to singing along with one or the other of them. They made such a rumpus that it got quite impossible. Besides, Nikolái Ivánovich suddenly got into a fierce argument with the waiters about the cigars, and it looked like there was a threat of a real awful hand-to-hand grabble. He asked for something called "Bueno-Gusto" and they lit it for him. Then when he asked for the box, the inscription turned out to be "Gueno Busto" or something even worse. Nikolái Ivánovich took all the cigars, tore them to bits, threw them on the floor, and stamped on them. This was the sort of thing he usually did to start a grabble.

'At that point, to prevent matters from coming to blows, a German or Jew appeared from behind the buffet and began scolding him in French. But when money was concerned, he didn't want to be bothered with French; he thumbed his nose and asked in German, "Habensi gelooked at that?"

' "That is, you mean to say you won't pay?"

' "No," he said. "Give me the bill."

'When they handed him the bill, he wouldn't take it. "This bill is padded," he said.

'He started checking it. "What's this written here, '*salade avec homards*'? I didn't order that . . . 'Pickles capuchon' – we never had them."

'The Jew said to him in Russian, "Oh yes, you did, sir! That way you could say you didn't have any of it."

' "No," he said. "You can't talk to me like that! I'll pay for what I saw on the table. Here on the table I see a fish, and you can do with it whatever you wish, but I'll pay for it. As for the consummation, we didn't have it, but you put it on the bill and I won't pay for it."

' "What consummation . . . ? It's not on the bill at all."

' "Well, that doesn't matter, you added something else."

'He got into such a fight that you couldn't do anything with him; he wouldn't pay a cent.

'So I told the boss, "Be good enough to let him alone right now . . . He's in a state now, but tomorrow send him the bill at the storeroom. In general he is a very proper gentleman."

'The Jew replied, "We know that in general he is a very proper gentleman, but then why is he so bad about paying his bills?"

'But they let him go anyway. I thought that at last we would get him out in peace, but no, out in the porter's lodge he was about to give the porter a small tip when he got into another argument. "These aren't my galoshes," he said. "Mine had high heels and carved tops!" He made a terrible racket and put all his change back in his pocket, didn't give the porter anything, and went off.

'Out in the air he started dozing off and kept crossing himself, half-asleep, repeating, "Sane Pete, Sane Pete." I gave him a few pokes to see if he was really dead, and he came to.

' "I was afraid you were dead," I said.

' "I was afraid too," he said. "I seemed to have the ace and queen of splades and the king of drymonds."

' "Oho!" I thought. "Now you've started to babble nonsense."

' "Nikolái Ivánovich," I said, "lean out the window. You need some fresh air."

'He did so, took a deep breath and said, "Yes, I feel better now . . . There's no more hic-scents in the air. The fuddle-drummers and saloon-players must have gone away. The little shops are already opening. Thank the Lord, it's morning! Here's the item on the gender now: you get out of the carriage and walk home; I am going alone outside the city gates and have some tea in a regular tavern."

61

' "Why don't you have your tea at home?" I said.

' "No, no, no," he answered. "What kind of a domestic-affairs lawyer are you? I want to go outside the gates; I'm going to meet the professor there and take up an entirely different item on the gender with him with regard to Arius."

' "How about signing this letter?" I said.

'He told me to go to the devil. I even burst into tears. What was I to do? Everything I had endured that night had apparently gone up in smoke. I tried to wheedle him – I even kissed his hand, but what was that to him?

' "Don't make me late," he said. "Here's a ruble for you. Go into that little shop and have the clerk sign for me. They do things like that." And he kicked me right out of the carriage.

'I got out and went into the shop. The clerk crossed himself and said, "You are the first customer, God bless you." But he wouldn't sign for Nikolái Ivánovich. "Of course," he said, "this is an unimportant matter, but right now we are afraid of the police and we don't even keep ink in the shop."

'Fortunately for me, a palm-reader came rushing in at that point wanting to buy the sourest kvas they had, and he advised me to hop over to the church and see the sextant who signs the holy bread. He was sure to sign it. He did sign it, but the idiot added some unnecessary words: "Nikolái Stépenev *and all his kin.*"

'To make matters worse, I didn't look it over until later. I had had enough and was fagged out. I put the letter in my bosom and went home. There I described all the antics of his majesty, beginning with Márya Amourovna, to his sisters, but I swore them to secrecy. Then I said, "Figure out yourselves what to do with him."

'Margaríta Mikháilovna, however, couldn't make up her mind yet; she was still in an indefinitive mood, thinking it would be enough if she took back the power of attorney she had given him. "But by the way," she added, "if Klávdinka won't give up this life of simplicity of hers and still insists on marrying the Reformist, then I'll agree; go and ask *him* to come."

'They called Klávdinka.

' "Klávdia! Maybe you thought things over last night and won't insist any more that Versteht's brother is the man who suits your ideas. If you have, tell me, and we won't send Márya Martýnovna."

'Klávdia answered in her usual caressing way, "No, Mama dear. I cannot give up that idea. He is an honest and good man, and I love him because with him I could pursue in harmony the same aim in life."

' "What is this aim of your life? Not to care for yourself, but only for others?"

' "Yes, Mama, to care not only for yourself, but for others as well."

' "That is meddling where you're not wanted."

'Then Margaríta Mikháilovna turned to me and said, "In that case, Márya Martýnovna, go ahead."

'At that for the first time in my life I saw Klávdinka cross herself up. She was a tight-lipped one all right, but she blushed and said, "Mama! If you are sending off this strange expedition for my sake, then let me assure you it will come to nothing."

' "Never mind, never mind. Let it go."

' "But darling, nothing at all will come of it."

' "Well, we'll see about that. Other people have benefited by it, and it will help us too. Go ahead, Márya Martýnovna."

'Klávdinka pleaded with her some more to give it up, but her mother answered, "Really, what business is it of yours? I only want to do some outstanding praying for myself! I trust I have the right to do that?"

' "All right, Mama, as you please!" replied Klávdinka, and went off to her room to mold some more forest sprites. I went off to do the will of him who sent me. I thought it would be simple to arrange everything here, just as you hope to now.'

'Don't you bother yourself about me!' returned Aíchka. 'I am a bold girl and I know why I can afford to be bold; I'm not afraid to spend money. If I want anyone, I make them come to me; if I want to go anywhere, I take a first-class ticket in a compartment.'

'Well, I don't know how much you intend to spend, but even with money you sometimes have to eat crow.'

'Oh no, with money you can tell anyone "habenzi gelooked".'

'No, when they get hold of you, you won't "gelook" at any more of it.'

'How are they going to get my own money away from me?'

'Yes, yes, yes! Anyway, I started off then, thinking everything would go very easily.'

'What made it so hard?'

'There's not a single person on earth who can imagine everything that can happen at a big expectension.'

'Don't keep beating around the bush and trying to show off how much you can do for me. Tell me what outstanding things happened to you.'

' "Habenzi" – you'll see.'

'Now listen, don't you dare talk to me like that. I don't like it.'

'Why not?'

'Because don't you repeat my jokes, but tell me how you came here and what started after that.'

'Well, the Bassompierres started.'

'Wait a minute. "The Bassompierres started." What on earth are Bassompierres? You look like you are mad at me. Well, don't sulk and also don't talk to me in an angry voice. With my money I'm not afraid of anything. I didn't insult you, and I don't like to spoil people who are my servants. Tell me now, what are Bassompierres?'

'People called that.'

'Well, tell me about them.'

Poor Márya Martýnovna sighed, and swallowing half her sigh, continued her story.

7

'It was here my real troubles began,' said Márya Martýnovna as she took up her story again. 'Right from the beginning. I had no sooner got off the train and started walking than I ran into a real fine man, a cab-driver. He was an easygoing chap, but a great talker – he was really good at that. As soon as he saw I didn't know my way around here, he bowed to me and said, "Having offered you my best wishes, may I make bold to inquire whether you intend going to hear the singer or to the Expectension?"

'I didn't even understand him and said, "Who is this singer? Why should I go hear him?"

' "He does everything with a chord," he replied.

'What the cabman said was undoubtedly very useful and fine, but I didn't understand what he meant by "a chord"; so I said, "I only want to know where the expectants gather."

' "Absolutely nothing will come of it. You'd better have the singer make you a chord, since he always accompanies *him* and is always at his elbow," said the cabman quietly.

'"Well," I said, "he must be some sort of sharper. I don't want to have anything to do with the likes of him, and I don't intend to take your advice."

'"Well, get in," he said. "For twenty kopecks I'll take you to the Expectension."

'He brought me here honestly, but when I got here, the place seemed to have a peculiar air about it. I didn't find anybody downstairs but the boy who unsticks the stamps from envelopes. I asked him, "Where does the audience take place?"

'"Here," he answered in a whisper.

'"And where are the grown-ups?"

'He didn't know. No matter what I asked him, he didn't know. He had apparently been drilled not to say too much.

'"And why," I asked, "are you collecting all those stamps? Can you answer that one?"

'He could. "For that they give you a bottle of oil and a package of tea in Jerusalem," he replied.

'"A clever lad," I thought, "quite the business man." But anyway, instead of listening to his childish conversation I would do better to go to church and see if the audience was being held there and incidentally say a prayer to the holy icon.

'I saw a crowd of people around the church who I took to be in a state of expectension too. Some other people kept going up to them and going away again and whispering. They looked exactly like plain-clothes defectives. That's what I took them for right off, and I thought perhaps that here too they were taking monumentary pictures of the passers-by, but later I found out that they were a local breed of Bassompierres. One of the ones walking around was a man of arthlectic build with a terribly outstanding knobby nose. He came up to me and asked in a pumpous tone, "On whose recommendation are you here and where are you staying?"

' "What kind of a cross-examination is this?" I replied. "What business is it of yours?"

' "Of course it's our business," he answered. "We are Moiséi Kartónych's men and we stay close to *him*."

' "Shoo! Now who on earth is Moiséi Kartónych and what does he count for?"

' "Aha!" he said. "So you don't know yet what he counts for! Then listen: he sits on heron eggs in a swamp and raises live cranes."

'I told him I wasn't interested and asked if he knew where the leash-holder was. He nodded his head toward the church.

' "Will vespers be over soon?" I asked.

' "This isn't vespers for us; this is midnight mass."

' "That can't be," I said. "There is no outstanding holiday tomorrow."

' "There isn't for you, but there is for us."

' "What holiday is it for you?"

' "To tell the truth," he said, "I don't know exactly. It's either the Seven Sleeping Maidens or the decrepitation of St Cropius' head."

' "Well," I said, "I see that even though you seem to be expecting something in front of a holy place, you are really crooks."

' "Yes, yes," he replied, "and now, with my best wishes, you beat it if you don't want to get thrashed."

'I didn't say any more and went into the church. I stood through the service, but even there I kept noticing defectives whispering among themselves. I began to worry that when everyone crowded up to the holy image they would certainly grab my money. I went out, came back here, and took a room almost like this one, but much, much smaller, for two rubles. I saw all sorts of different people in the corridor and I began listening to what they said. There was an officer who had come from Tashként and brought his wife from there; she had suffered an unimaginable misfortune. They were riding on a camel cart in a terrible heat. The camel walked unevenly, jerking all the time, and she was feeding a baby at the breast, and on account of the rough ride the milk in her breasts fermented into koumiss! The baby died of the koumiss, but she didn't want to bury it in the sand, and because of that a sort of craziness came over her. These people wanted to receive the very first blessing the next day and as much money as possible. I mean to say, naturally, the crazy woman wasn't trying to get it herself, but her husband was. To tell the truth, he was an unpleasant-looking man, with red eyes, and he kept playing up to everybody here, trying to get them to arrange a grant for him. He kept wheedling them, "Try your best, and we'll go halves on what God grants." But they would have nothing to do with him. Why go halves, when everybody would be glad to get it all for himself! Well, since I didn't intend to ask for any monetary blessings from him, I was puffed up with conceit and thought, "What do I care? I don't need any help!" I hoped to take it all in with my female brain and so gain an outstanding end of my expectension. But who had the real power and what the most outstanding thing was – that I didn't understand.'

'And what was the most outstanding thing?' inquired Aíchka curiously.

'Try and guess.'

'I don't like guessing, but wouldn't it most likely be the blessing?'

'Exactly right: the blessing, but what sort of blessing? Anyone can say "blessing", but not everybody understands just what this blessing consists of. You must have studied sacred history, haven't you?'

'I did, but I've forgotten everything.'

'How could you? It is unthinkable to forget everything.'

'Well, that's what I did.'

'Well, you remember Esau and Jacob. God discriminated between them when they were still in the womb: he loved Jacob and hated Esau.'

Aíchka burst out laughing.

'What are you laughing at, darling?'

'What sort of tales are you spinning me?'

'Oh no, pardon me. Those are no tales.'

'Do you think I don't understand? In his mother's womb a baby doesn't eat or drink anything; he only sweats. So what reason could there be for loving one and hating the other? The mother might hate them if she was ashamed of being pregnant, but what does God care about that?'

'Well, why God took a dislike for Esau – you ask the priests about that, not me. But the first blessing is always the most outstanding. Jacob put sheepskin stocking feet on his hands and grabbed the first blessing for himself, and Esau was left with the second. The second blessing can't be compared to the first. In this place here people have noticed that the most outstanding thing is to get hold of *him* as early as possible. Then you'll get your wish: money as well as a Bethluenza cure. But the later ones are all weaker. "His power departeth and consulteth."'

'Now I remember studying about that somewhere,' Aíchka put in.

'Well, I may not have studied about it, but I took up my petition ahead of the others and put it down. But the leash-holder pushed me back and said, "Please don't be forward." However, *he* read my letter and said, "Are you Stépeneva or not?"

' "No, father," I said. "I am a simple woman."

' "They are all simple people," he interrupted. "But there are some Stúpins or Stúkins besides."

' "No," I answered, "I'm not one of them. I come from the Stépenevs. It's an outstanding household."

' "Who is sick in their family?"

' "No one is sick," I replied. "They are all in good health, thank God."

' "Then what is your request?"

' "I was sent here," I answered, "to invite you to come and see them. They want to make a contribution to your good works."

' "All right," he said. "I will be there the day after tomorrow. You may expect me."

'I received his blessing and took the first train back in great expectension. My heart was filled with the joy of victory: I hadn't bowed down to anyone and hadn't given anything to the singer or the wringer or the leash-holder and had managed everything just fine. I kept chattering like a magpie to the people going back with me, telling them he would visit us first two days later and that he had ordered me to meet him in a carriage. They asked me what fortunate family I belonged to. In my simplicity I didn't suspect anything and like a fool told them all frankly my own family was insignificant, but that the happy family was that of those outstanding merchants, the Stépenevs. Then an argument started about whether they were really an outstanding family or not.

'There was only one cook who stood up for them. "I know some fruit-dealers named Stépenev," he said, "and they are outstanding: I lost my place at the general's on account of them – they passed off some fake cheese on me."

'The other passengers pretended they had never heard of any Stépenevs. I foolishly went and gave them all the particulars, not having the slightest idea what lengths human nastiness could go to and what would come of it.'

'What did come of it?' drawled Aíchka.

'Oh, there was a great hullaballoon. Suddenly the officer from Tashként rushed at me and started shouting, "Shut up, you loud-mouthed imbecile! I can't stand listening to you, you irritate me! I don't believe that man is a saint at all. I spent twelve rubles coming to see him with my sick wife, and he only gave me ten rubles! What business! He takes in money like drinking from a trough, but when he gives it out he dribbles it through his fingers. And his henchmen keeping sounding their horns and printing rubbish. It's a bazaar!"

'At his yelling they all quieted down, because he had an awfully greedy look about him. He tossed two rolls to his wife like he was throwing them to a dog; he himself walked around and rolled his eyes in all directions.

' "Don't answer him," the others said quietly. "He's a putriot who goes in for machicanery."

'But there was a shopkeeper who recognized him and explained, "He is no putriot; he's a swindler. That wretched woman he takes along as his wife is not his wife at all, but an idiot girl from a wayside inn."

'And sure enough, as soon as we arrived and started getting out, two policemen came up to him and took him off to the station; the woman's relatives had been searching for her.

'We all let out a great sigh: Oh, oh, oh! What infamy! What treachery! And we were all amazed that *he* hadn't seen through him at all. Then we got scared. After all, how could you see through anyone in that hubbub? So we scattered, each to his own house.

'When I arrived home, I went straight to Margaríta Mikháilovna and said, "Sign yourself with the cross and rejoice: God has been merciful. The day after tomorrow it will be our turn to celebrate and happiness will dawn upon you. I obtained his consent and in the morning I must go to meet him in expectension."

'They were both delighted – Margaríta Mikháilovna and Efrosínya Mikháilovna – and they began to question me as to whether I had found out how they should receive him and present their request. I told them I had found out everything, but that nothing specially outstanding was needed, only tea with plain white rolls and grapes; if he should agree to stay for a meal, they could give him giblet soup.

' "Maybe we ought to have some first-rate wine?"

' "The only wine you can serve him," I said, "is first-class Madeira. But the most important thing for you to decide right now is who is to go meet him – you yourself or me or Nikolái Ivánovich, if he's in his right mind. In my opinion Nikolái Ivánovich would be the best, since he is a man and the outstanding member of the household. Only let's hope he isn't in one of his crazy moods right now."

'They decided that Nikolái Ivánovich and I should go together; somehow we would manage to keep him under control until then. Nikolái Ivánovich was to ride back with him from there in the carriage, and I would come back in a cab.

'Fortunately for us Nikolái Ivánovich appeared that evening in a state of penitence and oblivion. He walked along waving his arms in front of him and muttering, "A path, a path . . . goes the voice, crying prepare him a way in the wilderness . . . O Lord!"

'Then he plumped down in a corner and began searching through his pockets. I went up to him and said, "What are you looking for – the day you wasted yesterday? Go up and take a rest right now."

' "Wait a minute," he replied. "I had a very important objective in my pocket, and it's not there now."

' "What objective?"

' "Tverdamáskov made me an experimental portrait of
Krutílda in undressabillé and I wanted to keep it so as not
to show it to anybody, and now I have lost it. I don't like the
idea of people looking it over. I am going out and hunt for it."

' "Now don't you do that," I said. "Now you're home, you
hush up. You're not going out again." So we locked him up
for two days to make him come to his senses.

'The night after that I slept like I was in paradise, with ether-
eal angels flying all around me; you couldn't see their faces,
but how they did flap their wings!'

'What did they look like?' Aíchka inquired with curiosity.

'They were like church singers with their investments and
surpluses on. But when the dream was over and a new day
began, my troubles started up again. Early in the morning
we began bustling around, arranging everything for the next
day. They were afraid to take a step without me. I had to go
with Efrosínyushka to the fowlery and pick out the giblets
for the soup – they had to be outstanding ones – and I helped
keep an eye on Nikolái Ivánovich. The next day, when we
were to meet him, I got up before it was light and ran to the
coachman Mirón to have him do a good job of harnessing
the carriage.

'He was a terrible rough one and an artful answerer and he
couldn't stand taking orders from women. Whatever you said
to him, he always had a cutting reply ready for you: "I know
it all figuratively myself."

' "Now don't you be coarse with me," I told him. "You
do a good job with the harnessing – this is an outstanding
event."

' "Nothing stands out any more. I don't care what you say; I'll put the harness on according to form, and that's all."

'I was still more worried that Klávdinka might leave the house without me and make a skeptacle of herself, because we all knew she had no religion. I told Margaríta Mikháilovna, "Take care, ma'am, that she doesn't pull off something outstanding on you."

'So Margaríta Mikháilovna said to her, "Klavdyúsha, please don't go anywhere today."

' "All right, Mother," she replied. "Why should I go anywhere if you don't want me to?"

' "But you don't believe in anything, do you?"

' "Who ever told you that kind of nonsense, Mama dear, and why did you believe it?" Margaríta Mikháilovna was overjoyed. "Then you really do believe in something?"

' "Of course I do, Mama."

' "What is it you believe in?"

' "That there is a God and that Jesus Christ lived on this earth and that we should live as His Gospel teaches."

' "You believe that truly – you are not lying to me?"

' "I never lie, Mama."

' "Swear it."

' "Mama, I never swear; the Gospel forbids us to swear."

' "Why shouldn't you swear for the sake of your mother's peace of mind?" I put in.

'She didn't so much as answer me a word, but her mother kissed her joyfully and said, "She never lies and I believe her without any oath. You all want me not to believe her."

' "How can you say that?" I replied. "I believe anything you want me to."

'But I thought to myself, "When *he* comes all this faith of hers will be put to the test. There is no point in splitting hairs with her now." So I rushed off again to see to Mirón's harnessing. He had already harnessed the horses and brought up the carriage, but he was dressed in an ordinary peasant coat.

' "Why didn't you put on your best coat?" I stormed.

' "Sit down, sit down," he replied. "It's none of your affair. The best coat is only for winter."

'I saw he was in a nasty mood.

'Nikolái Ivánovich meekly got into the carriage by me; the two ladies stayed home to get things ready for us. Meanwhile we had such outstanding adventures that they surpassed anything that happened to Esau and Jacob.'

'What happened?' exclaimed Aíchka.

'The most outstanding first blessing was snatched away from us.'

'In what manner?'

'That is where Moiséi Kartónych comes in!'

8

'So Nikolái Ivánovich and I rode up in the carriage. He had all his appurtenances on – his church-elder medal around his neck and a foreign order, the gift of the Shah. I was dressed as usual, modestly, as befits my station, nothing outstanding, but clean and neat. There was an impenetrable mob of people and several carriages standing in expectension. Some of them had ordinary horses and some of them had their manes clipped; there were grooms on the boxes with cracking-whips. Policemen were engaged in hand-to-hand grabble with everyone – they wanted to make them stand in line, but they couldn't.

'The assistant inspector was jumping up and down like a frightened sparrow and pleading with the crowd. "Ladies and gentlemen! Don't be disorderly . . . ! You will all have a chance to see him. Why this lack of culture?"

' "Here's a man of education!" I thought. I went up to him and asked him to have our carriage put ahead of the others, because we had been assigned the first audience, but a lot of help he was! He didn't pay any attention to all my persuasive words, but ruffled up his sparrow feathers and said, "What outcasts of Christianity! What swinish lack of culture!"

'Suddenly I noticed among the raffle that all my acquaintances of three days before had gathered there – the ones I came back on the train with – and especially the pious old woman whose whole family was down with Bethluenza. So I had a talk with her.

' "So you're here," she said.

' "Naturally I'm here," I replied. "We were promised the first audience."

' "You're from the Stépenevs, is that right?"

' "Yes," I replied. "I'm from the Stépenevs, in their carriage. This is Mirón, our coachman."

' "Oh," she said. "Mirón the coachman . . ."

'Suddenly all the people gave a start and started making the sign of the cross and trampling on one another mercilessly, like a drove of wild horses trying to crush each other. There was such an uproar of groaning and squealing that, to tell the truth, it sounded like all the people had turned into beasts and were trying to strangle each other!

'The assistant inspector couldn't even yell any more, he only groaned, "What outcasts of Christianity! What cattle without reason or pity!" The policemen were about to go into grabble again, but suddenly those burbondy faces crowded through from somewhere – the ones I had seen here, the Bassompierres who talked about the Sleeping Maidens. They scattered the whole mob at a stroke, policemen, expectants, and all! How they did scatter them! They grabbed hold of *him* and pushed him over toward some other carriages, yelling, "This way! This way!" I even heard them mention the Stépenevs, but in the meantime they put him into somebody else's carriage and carried him off.

'I put up a shout, "Wait a minute! this is unthinkable – that's not the Stépenevs' carriage . . . Our coachman is named Mirón!"

'By that time they had treacherously put him into the other carriage, with that very old woman, my pious fellow-traveler, whose family were all down with Bethluenza, and they took him off to her house.'

Aíchka intervened and said, 'What is it? That's the way it should be.'

'Why?'

'She had a sick family on her hands, and you didn't.'

Martýnovna did not try to dispute this and went on with her story.

'I went up to the inspector and said, "For heaven's sake, Colonel, how can you allow such disorder!"

' "And what have they done to you?" he came back at me. "You heathen! You did more shoving than anyone else. What happened, did somebody step on your favorite corn? There's an apothecary's, go in and get yourself a plaster."

' "The point is not the apothecary's," I said, "but that I was assigned the first audience, and she wasn't."

' "Why didn't you grab hold of it then, this audience of yours?"

' "I would have, but the police didn't keep order. You saw it yourself, that it was unthinkable for me to get up to him; they grabbed away . . ."

' "What did they grab from you?"

' "They pushed me back . . ."

' "But you had nothing stolen?"

' "No, not stolen, but there was cheating with the audiences."

'At that he waved his hand. "That's of no importance!" he said. "That often happens." And he wouldn't pay any more attention to me.

' "That's enough of you," he said. "Move along."

'I went back to Nikolái Ivánovich, who had settled down in the carriage, and told him, "What's the use of staying here? We've got to chase after them in a hurry and at least get the second audience."

'He answered that he "didn't care", but Miróshka put up an argument right off.

' "We can't chase after them," he said.

' "But you can still see them there on the bridge. Start after them and you'll catch up with them right away."

' "I can't chase after them."

' "And why not? You have always been a continual boor and an artful answerer."

' "That's just it," he replied. "I am an answerer. I'll have to answer for it. You'll be sitting in the carriage, but for that they'll formidably remove me from my box and put me behind bars in the police station. It's not allowed to chase after people at full speed."

' "Then why is that carriage there going after them in such a hurry?"

' "Because those horses are different."

' "What's the matter with ours? How are they any worse?"

' "They're not worse, but those are English racers and ours are Tambóv duffers, and there's a difference."

' "You may be an artful answerer, you've got an answer for everything, but the real reason is that their coachman is a better driver."

' "Why shouldn't he be a better driver, when their house-keeper in front of everyone gave him a whole bottle of cherry licker, and at home they don't even give me brown bread to drink with my tea."

' "You go as fast as he does and I'll give you a whole bottle of licker when we get home."

' "In that case," he said, "take your formidable seat as quickly as you can."

'I got back in the carriage and we started off. Mirón kept up with them: wherever they went with their racers, we were after them with our duffers – we didn't lag behind. But whenever I looked out the window, it seemed to me that all the carriages going along with us were in expectension too. I counted seven carriages, and in the eighth I saw two ladies sitting and called to them, "Keep back, if you please, this is my audience."

'Suddenly Nikolái Ivánovich pulled me back with all his might, made me sit down, and hissed at me in a stifled nasty voice, "Don't you dare yell like that! I'm ashamed to be with you."

' "For heaven's sake!" I said. "What shame can there be with this shameless raffle?"

' "That is no raffle," he replied, "that's a blonde I know; through a certain person she could put a very unpleasant item on the gender for me."

'Then he gave me such a tug that my dress ripped. I got

mad and smacked him on the hand and struck the door with my elbow. I hit the glass so hard that it shattered into smithereens.

'A policeman galloped up to us and said, "Allow me to inquire what you mean by this scene of violence? What is that lady so noisy about?"

' "Leave us," he said. "This lady is not in her right mind; I am taking her to the madhouse for a testimonial."

'The policeman said, "In that case go along!"

'So we chased off again, but just then we were cut off by a funeral procession. As if to spite us they were just taking some regimental corpse to be buried with a parade. There was a great lot of clergy, all walking by pairs in line, one after the other, with the archbishop behind. Then came the coffin. Then the soldiers shuffled by at great length, bringing up the rear with two cannons, as if they were going to make a fire on the crowd. After that there was no end to the carriages, most of them empty. Well, by the time all that had passed before our eyes, *he* had naturally gone and the racers were nowhere to be seen.

'We started off again, but we didn't know where to go. Luckily just then a man appeared from somewhere and said, "Command me to get up on the box with the coachman; I am a co-pursuer, and I know where the first audience is."

'We gave him a ruble, and he got up and we started off. I hadn't the slightest idea where we were going. The Stépenevs' house is in the Yamskáya village, but we had arrived at the grain wharves, where we really found a huge crowd of people gathered and standing in expectension . . . I was even scared to look, there were so many! We couldn't see *him* at all – he had got out of the carriage and, so they said, had been taken by force into the house to rescue him from the expectants. Now the doors had been closed behind him, and two policemen were stationed there and wouldn't let anyone in. If anyone got rough, they would grab him and take him away.

'Actually, however, all the expectants were behaving themselves very well, waiting and talking about his various miracles, mostly about winnings at cards and Bethluenza. Suddenly my master Nikolái Ivánovich flew into a rage.

' "Why should I stand here with you bigots?" he said. "I don't have the Bethluenza and besides, they might take me for a bankrupt! I don't want to fool around here with you any more waiting here. Stay here with the carriage and wait, and I'll take an ordinary cab and go off where I please."

'I tried to argue him out of it. "All are equal," I said, "in the eyes of God. This is the expectension of God. If you wish to be deemed worthy of something outstanding, then you must wait patiently."

'Somehow he agreed, reluctantly, to wait for one hour, and he marked off the time on his watch.

'During the hour we suffered through there I almost talked my tongue off trying to persuade Nikolái Ivánovich to stay. I was talking so hard I didn't notice that someone had come out of the entrance. That very second *he* was plunked into another carriage and rushed off to another audience. My God! Another sly trick! How could you stand it! We went after him again, and the third time we had the same success as before, because Nikolái Ivánovich with all his medals and appurtenances wouldn't come out where people could see him, but hid in the carriage. I looked too common, and they kept pushing me away.

'At long last Nikolái Ivánovich said, "Now you keep quiet! I don't intend to be the last man in the suite any more. You can sit here and follow him, but I'm through with it."

'With that he took off all his appurtenances and hid them in his pocket.

' "Good Lord," I said. "How can I stay here alone? It is unthinkable!"

'But suddenly he got rambunctious and said, "You stay and think about what is thinkable and what is unthinkable, and I'll go have some vodka and a bite of lamprey in the tavern."

' "Wait a while more," I said. "Pray to God with your fast unbroken and then eat. Everything is ready at home – not only lamprey, but all sorts of fish, and outstanding giblets and other appurtenances."

'He actually told me to go to the devil. "A lot I need that!" he said; "I saw what your outstanding giblets are like!" But instead of going into the tavern, he took a cab and went off altogether.

'At that I actually burst out crying. I had taken a lot of base-ness from people in my life, but how could I have imagined such outstanding vileness as that: they had dragged *him* off by force and by using someone else's name had lured him into the wrong carriage and carried him off.

'In my despair I told some others what had been done. They weren't surprised and said, "Don't feel bad. They often do that with him."

'As soon as he came out, I saw the same ones who had been so glib with their tongues rush at him like tigers, right before my eyes. For the fourth time they grabbed hold of him, pushed him into a carriage and carried him off.

'I simply dissolved in tears and shouted to Miróshka, "Mirón, my boy, keep the love of God in your heart and drive those duffers of yours without pity. I've got to get to that fifth audience ahead of the others. Go at a gallop and don't let anyone pass you! I'll give you two bottles of licker!"

' "All right!" answered Mirón. "I'll give them a formidable rein!" And he whipped up the duffers with all his might so they ran faster than the racers. At one point we knocked an old woman off her feet and made a quick turn into a side alley. They caught up again and when the first carriage started making the turn, Mirón cut out in front of it and broke something off their vehicle. The two carriages hooked together, pulling theirs over on its side. Ours only creaked with the strain.

'The coachmen started swearing at each other. The policemen grabbed our horses by the bridles and started writing down Mirón's address.

'Just then *he* came out again, but this time I flung open the carriage doors and went right up to him. "I beg your pardon," I said, "but did you not deign to promise to come to see us today? We are the Stépenevs, merchants . . . They are outstanding people and have been in general expectention since early morning."

'He looked at me like a very tired or greatly surprised pigeon and said, "What is the meaning of this? I have been at the Stépenevs' today."

' "When?" I said. "Have mercy! No, you haven't been there."

'He took out his notebook and looked in it to make sure.

' "The Stépenevs?"

' "Yes, sir."

' "Merchants?"

' "Outstanding merchants."

' "Yes, here they are . . . outstanding . . . I have them crossed off . . . Their name is crossed off in my notebook. So I have been at the Stépenevs'."

' "No," I said. "I beg your pardon. This is unthinkable. I haven't left you for a minute since early morning."

' "But I went to the Stépenevs' the very first. I remember the family: an old woman in a dark dress took me there."

'I guessed who that old woman was! It was the one I had talked to about the outstanding family of the Stépenevs.

' "There has been treachery perpetuated," I said. "She didn't come from the Stépenevs' at all; the Stépenevs don't even live where you were."

'He merely raised one shoulder and said, "Well, what can we do about it? You wait here a little. I'll settle things here and go with you."

'So I was left waiting again, this time for the sixth audience. I realized for the first time that there were people in the world like these Bassompierres! A whole guild of them had been collected; their master was the one who had made fun of me with the Seven Sleeping Maidens, the one with the arthlectic build and the outstanding nose. Vagabonds they were, guttersnipes, lazy idlers who wouldn't work. The only job they had was to keep watch and suddenly to crowd close together and not let anybody through. If you gave them something, they would stick him into your carriage, but if you didn't, they'd move back and . . .'

'Don't say it,' joked Aíchka.

'I'm mum. Later on an old woman told me, "Why do you follow him around like a fool? Can't you see who is running this show? Call over that man in the green blouse and give him something for his pains – he'll squeeze him right to you. That's their only bread and butter."

'I beckoned to this industrial individual and gave him a ten-kopeck piece. But he was a sober lad, and not satisfied with my ten kopecks, asked for a ruble. I gave him a ruble; he cleared a pathway to our carriage, pushed and shoved, and finally squeezed him right up to the door, shouting, "Good luck!"

'So I got him and took him off.'

9

'I meant to ride separately from him, thinking myself unworthy to sit by him, but he was very unassuming and invited me in himself.

' "Let's sit together," he said. "It's all right."

'He is very simple and direct, even though he is an out-standing figure.'

Márya Martýnovna's audience interrupted her and asked, 'Where does his figure stand out?'

To tell the truth, I was also curious to hear that, but the narrator avoided answering it and said, 'You'll see for yourself tomorrow.' Then she went on:

'I sat on the front seat and looked at him. I saw that he was completely exhausted. The poor darling was yawning and kept taking letters out of his pocket. He had a tremendous lot of letters in his pocket, and he kept fishing them out and spreading them on his lap. He crumpled up the money as if it didn't mean anything to him and put it carelessly back in his pocket without counting it, because he never keeps any of it for himself.'

'How do you know that?' drawled Aíchka.

'Oh, my dear, it's even a sin to doubt it; God will punish you for that.'

'I don't doubt it, but I'm only curious . . . They say people steal from him – who knows?'

'I don't think so – I never heard about it.'

'But I have.'

'Oh well, he probably made up the difference out of his own money.'

'That's just it.'

'Oh well, that's clear. He's not interested in it . . . So he would open a letter, read it, put the money in his pocket and make a mark with his pencil. Then he would open another and in the meantime he kept joking with me just as friendly as you please.'

'What did he joke about, for instance?'

'Well, for instance he asked me, "What's the meaning of this? Is it true that I haven't been at the Stépenevs'?"

' "You certainly haven't," I said.

'He shook his head, smiled and laughed, "Maybe you are taking me there for the second time?"

' "For mercy sakes," I said. "That would be unthinkable."

' "With you," he replied, "everything is thinkable."

'Then he went on reading and reading and said again, "But who was that then if it wasn't the Stépenevs? Because of this mix-up I don't know whom to cross off in my book."

'I realized he was annoyed, but I didn't know what to say.'

Aíchka interrupted, 'How can he be a saint, when he doesn't see what is being done with him?'

'Well, you see, he supposed that the Stépenevs were the people where he had been taken first by treachery. They asked him to help their son, who is a terrible hell-raiser; he had made friends with a frivolous woman and wanted to get married. He wouldn't have anything to do with any other prospective brides of good family.'

'Why was that?' asked Aíchka.

'You see, he felt a duty, an obligation to restrain her in a moderate life.'

'More likely he just fell in love with her beauty.'

'Of course . . . There was something outstanding . . . But I brought the conversation back to my own problems. I told him that the real Stépenevs didn't have an outstanding son . . .

' "And what does the unoutstanding one do?"

'I replied that they didn't have an unoutstanding one either.

' "In other words, they have no son."

' "None at all."

' "Then why do you mix things up with 'outstanding' and 'unoutstanding'?"

' "Excuse me, that's just a saying of mine. The Stépenevs have a daughter, not a son, and the trouble is with her."

'He shook his head in a tired way and asked, "What is the trouble?"

' "The trouble is that she is the heiress to a fortune and young and beautiful, but she doesn't want to live as she ought to."

'Suddenly he caught on and remembered something. "The Stépenevs, you say . . . Wait, isn't Stúpin a brother of theirs?"

'I didn't understand, and he was perplexed.

' "We're going to the Stúpins' now, aren't we?"

' "No, to the Stépenevs'. The Stúpins are one thing, and the Stépenevs are another. See, here is their house with a signal on the gate, "Stépenev, merchants"."

'He looked sharply as if he had just remembered something he had forgotten and asked, "What is the signal for?"

' "It's the sign that marks the house."

' "Oh, a sign . . . Yes, I see it."

'Suddenly he collected all the unopened envelopes, put them in his inside pocket and started getting out at the entrance.

'There was a tremendous crowd of people in expectension at our door. The raffle blocked off the entire street, and besides there were four more carriages waiting behind us for an audience.

'We slammed the entrance door shut after him, but then an awfully annoying thing happened: an officer's wife who was trying forcibly to push her way into the house had two of her fingers crushed by some young lad and went into a kind of faint.

'We had just settled that when a policeman rang the bell to take Mirón to the station. They had to write a report on his running over the old woman and smashing someone's carriage. We hid Mirón in a hurry in the pantry room; I carried out my promise and gave him some licker. But inside the house there was something still more outstanding waiting for us.'

10

'Naturally he made a marvelous entrance, like goodness personified, and said, "Peace be with you all," and blessed everybody – the mistress Margaríta Mikháilovna and Efrosínya Mikháilovna and the older servants. But when it was Nikolái Ivánovich's turn, we discovered that that most noble gentleman was not at home. Then Mama and Auntie rushed off to Klávdinka's room. Klávdinka was at home all right, but, if you please, she had no intention of coming out for the service.

' "Where is your little daughter?" he asked.

'Poor Margaríta Mikháilovna, overcome with shame, answered, "She is home; she'll be right here!"

' "Right here" was a little strong when she wouldn't think of coming out.

'Before that she had been affectionate with her mother and had embraced her, not saying a word about not coming out. But now, when we had already arrived, her mother ran into her room beside herself, and said, "He's coming! He's coming!"

'Klávdinka answered her in a very calm voice, "Well, Mama, that's fine. I am glad this is going to be a pleasure for you."

' "Then come out and meet him and go up to him!"

'She only smiled that quiet smile of hers, but she wouldn't do it.

' "So you want to make trouble for me?" her mother said.

' "Not at all, Mama. I am very glad for you. You wanted to see him, and now your wish is being fulfilled."

' "I suppose for you it's not a pleasure?"

' "Mama dear, it's all the same to me."

' "Then how could you say that you believed in God?"

' "Of course I believe, Mama. I need no one besides Him."

' "But I suppose you don't need to observe any of the practices of the faith?"

' "I do observe them, Mama dear."

' "What do you observe?"

' "What is required of us all: to eat bread in the sweat of one's brow and not to do evil to anyone."

' "Ah, so that's what your beliefs are now! Then realize this: you are doing a great evil to me right now."

' "What evil? How can you say that, Mama? Well, forgive me."

' "No, no! You are disgracing me before all my family and before the whole town. What are you doing, getting ready to be a house painter or a laundress? What have you got all over yourself?"

'Klávdinka was kneading clay as she stood there.

' "Put away your modeling right now!"

' "Why do you want me to do that, Mama?"

' "Put it away! Put it away right now! And take off that apron of yours and come out with me, or else I'll tear your apron off by force, throw all that clay-modeling antillery on the floor, and trample it with my feet!"

89

' "Mama dear," she replied, "I'll do anything you please, but I can't come out."

' "Why not?"

' "Because I believe that all this is improper."

'At that her mother couldn't stand any more and – what had never happened with them – called her a bad name:

' "You're a villain! A viper!"

'Her daughter answered her with an affectionate reproach, "Mama dear! Mama! You will be sorry you said that later."

' "Come out right now!"

' "I can't."

' "You can't?"

' "I can't, Mama."

'Then her mother slammed her clay figure down on the floor and began trampling on it with her heels. When her daughter was about to embrace her and try to calm her down, Margaríta Mikháilovna flew into a fury and slapped her right in the face.'

'The statue?' asked Aíchka.

'No, my dear, Klávdinka herself.

' "Don't be sassy with me!"

'Klávdinka gasped and clasped her face with both hands, rocking on her feet.

'She should have tied her hands!' remarked Aíchka.

'No, she didn't do that. Klávdinka merely begged, "Mama dear! Have pity on yourself! This is terrible – why, you are a woman! You have never been like this!"

'Margaríta Mikháilovna, choking with rage, said, "No, I have never been like this, but now it's come out. It's you who have reduced me to this! And from now on you are not my daughter. I curse you, and I shall send a request to the commission to have you placed in an incorrigible institution."

'And so in such a situation, all upset and after such an exhibition, Margaríta Mikháilovna had to come out and meet *him*! You can imagine the outstanding lamentation!

'Apparently he didn't notice that there was anyone missing. He began saying prayers in front of the icons – he doesn't sing, but says it all from memory – but none of us prayed; we kept exchanging glances. The mother looked at her sister and made a sign for her to go and get Klávdinka. When Efrosínya came back she signaled that Klávdinka wouldn't come.

'Efrosínya went up for the second time, and the mother again kept watching the door after her. Again Efrosínya Mikháilovna came in alone and again made a sign that she wouldn't come.

'Her mother made a face, "Why not?"

'Margaríta Mikháilovna signaled to me, "Go and persuade her to come."

'I indicated that it was unthinkable.

'But she said "Please!" with her eyes and pointed to her dress, meaning, "I'll give you a dress."

'I went up. When I came in, Klávdinka was picking up the pieces of clay from the statute her mother had broken.

' "Klávdia Rodiónovna," I said. "Give up making a skeptacle of yourself. Be nice to your mother and go down; please go."

'She answered me in my own words, "Please go!"

'I said, "What a hard heart you have! You are sorry for outsiders, but here is a chance for you to be nice to your own mother, and you won't. You can at least do that even without any faith at all." '

'Of course,' confirmed Aíchka.

'Yes, naturally! Lord, no one believes everything the priests claim, but that doesn't make you hinder others from believing them.

'But as soon as I had finished giving her that bit of edify-ance, she ordered me, "Get out!" And what for? "Because," she said, "you are falsehood incarnate and you teach me to lie and pretend. I can't endure you: what you say to me is vile."

'I went back, and while I was explaining by signs all that had happened, I didn't notice that *he* had stopped reading and had gone over to the jardinary, broken off a stem from a flower and started sprinkling water with it. He thanked everyone, congratulated them, and didn't sing at all. Everything he did was somehow especially outstanding.

' "I thank you," he said, "for saying a prayer with me. But where are the other members of your family?"

'So they had to lie again: they lied about Nikolái Ivánovich, saying that he had been called to the count's on a commission.

' "And your daughter, where is she?"

'Well, at that Margaríta Mikháilovna couldn't stand it and burst out crying.

'Understanding, he caressed her like an angel and said, "Grieve not! Grieve not! In youth there is much that is unto-ward, but later they see what is good for them and leave their evil ways."

' "God grant it! God grant it!" said the old woman.

'He soothed her, saying, "Pray, believe, and hope, and she will be like all the others."

' "God grant it!" she said again.

' "And God will grant it! It shall be unto you according to your faith. But if she does not care to come out and see us now, perhaps I could go in and see her?"

'When she heard that, Margaríta Mikháilovna actually fell at his feet from gratitude, but he lifted her up and said, "What are you doing? What are you doing? It is meet to bow down to God alone, and I am a man."

'That instant Efrosínya Mikháilovna and I rushed off to Klávdinka's room and said, "Hurry! Hurry! You wouldn't come down to him, but he now desires to come and see you."

' "Well, what of it?" she replied calmly.

' "He wants to know whether you are willing to receive him."

' "This is Mama's house," replied Klávdinka. "In her house everyone may go where he pleases."

'I ran out and said, "Come in, please."

'He smiled sweetly at me in reply and said to Margaríta Mikháilovna, "I say unto you, be not cast down! I work no miracles, but if a miracle is needed, there have always been miracles, there are and ever shall be. Take me to her and leave us for a moment. I must speak with her in nothing but the omnipresence of God."

' "Of course! Heavens! Don't we understand? Only help us, Lord!" '

'Well, I couldn't have stood it,' said Aíchka. 'I would have eavesdropped.'

'You wait a minute. Don't get ahead of me.'

II

'We showed him to the door of Klávdinka's room and then ran around through the dining room, which had a window into her room over the door. Efrosínya and I climbed up on the table, but Margaríta Mikháilovna was too heavy and was afraid to climb onto the table; so she only stuck her ear up to the crack in the door and listened.

'As soon as he came in he put his hand on her head and said in priest style, "Good afternoon, my daughter."

'She calmly took his hand in hers, removed it from her head and simply shook it, replying, "Good afternoon."

'He wasn't offended, but from then on he spoke to her coolly and formally.

' "May I sit down and have a chat with you?"

' "If you like, sit down," she replied. "But don't get dirty. Your clothes are of silk, and there is clay here."

'He looked at the chair and sat down without noticing that he had accidentally knocked her little Gospel off it with his sleeve. Without any antecedent chit-chat he came out and asked her, "You are engaged in clay-modeling?"

' "Yes, I am," she replied.

' "Naturally, you do this out of desire rather than necessity?"

' "Both from desire and from necessity."

'He gave her an expressive look. "What necessity?"

' "Every person needs to work; that is his function and it is of benefit to him."

' "Yes, if it is not done to be fashionable, it is good."

' "Even if a person began to engage in labor in order to be fashionable and had not done so before, it would not be bad," she answered.

'You understand, things had taken such a turn that it seemed as though it was she who would offer *him* edifyance. But he started questioning her more sternly.

' "You seem weak and unhealthy to me."

' "No," she said, "I am quite healthy."

' "I am told you don't eat meat."

' "No, I don't."

' "Why not?"

' "I don't like it."

' "You don't like the taste?"

' "The taste, and I simply don't like to see corpses in front of me."

'He was amazed. "What corpses?" he asked.

' "The corpses of birds and animals," she replied. "The food that is put on the table is all made of their corpses."

' "What! A roast or gravy is corpses! What simplemindedness! And you have taken an oath to observe this for your entire life?"

' "I never take oaths."

' "Animals," he said, "are granted us to be used for food."

' "That's not my affair," she answered.

' "I suppose you wouldn't give meat to a sick person?" he said.

' "Why not? If he needed it, I would."

' "Then what would happen?"

' "Nothing."

' "And who taught you this?"

' "No one."

' "But how did it come into your head?"

' "Are you really interested?"

' "Very much! Because this foolishness is widespread now, and we must know it."

' "In that case I will tell you where I got this foolishness."

' "Please do."

' "I was living in the country with my nurse. There was no one to slaughter the chickens, so we didn't slaughter them. We lived and the chickens lived and I fed them and I saw that it was possible to live without slaughtering anybody and I liked it."

' "And if at that time a sick man had come to you for whom a chicken needed to be killed?"

' "I think that for a sick man I would have killed a chicken."

' "Yourself even!"

' "Yes, myself."

' "With these tender little hands of yours?"

' "Yes, with these hands of mine."

'He elevated his shoulders and said, "It is terrible how inconsistent you are!"

'She replied that to save a man you could even be inconsistent.

' "It's simply obscurantism! Perhaps you don't want to own property either?"

' "Under what circumstances?"

' "It's all the same."

' "No, it's not; if I have two dresses and someone else has none at all, then I don't want two dresses as my property."

' "So that's it!"

' "Yes, that is as it should be, according to the Scriptures."

'And with that she was pleased to stretch out her dainty hand toward the place where her little Gospel always lay, but it wasn't there, because he had accidentally knocked it off. He stopped her himself, saying, "It is vain for us to speak of this."

' "Why?"

' "Because your only desire is to prove the straight crooked."

' "And it seems to me that your only desire is to prove the crooked straight!"

' "That is all obscurantism in you," he said. "It is because you do not bear your familial responsibilities. Why are you still a maiden at your age?"

' "Because I am not married."

' "And why not?"

'She glared at him. "What do you mean, why not? Because I have no husband."

' "But perhaps you reject marriage?"

' "No, I do not reject it."

' "You acknowledge that the most important mission of a woman is to live for her family?"

' "No, I am of a different opinion," she replied.

' "What is your opinion?"

' "I think that to marry a worthy man is very good, but to remain a virgin and live for the good of others is still better than being married."

' "Why is that?"

' "Why do you ask me that? You must know the answer yourself: he who marries must take on cares in order to please his family, but a single person can have broader and higher cares than about his own family."

' "But those are mere words."

' "What do you mean, words?" she said. And again she moved her hand toward the table, but he stopped her and said, "Do not try to prove it. I know where these things are said, but you must be able to understand them. The human race must multiply in order to carry out its mission."

' "Well, and then?"

' "And children must be born."

' "And children are born."

' "And there must be someone to love and instruct them."

' "Yes! Yes! that is necessary."

' "And to love a child and care for its welfare is granted only to a mother's heart."

' "Not at all."

' "Then to whom?"

' "To any heart in which there is love of God."

' "You are in error: for a child no stranger's heart can replace his mother's."

' "Not at all. It is very difficult, but it is possible."

' "But one can work for the general welfare in wedlock as well."

' "Yes, but that is still more difficult than remaining unmarried."

' "So for you there is no joy in life."

' "Oh yes, there is."

' "What is it?"

' "To grow accustomed not to live for myself."

' "In that case it would be better for you to go into a convent."

' "Why should I do that?"

' "Everything is arranged there so as not to live for oneself."

' "I don't by any means think everything is arranged in that way there."

' "What do you know about life in convents?"

' "A good deal."

' "Where have you observed the monastic life?"

'But she cut him off, and said, "Excuse me . . . Isn't it enough that I answer all your questions about myself? I am not accustomed to telling stories about anyone else." And right in front of him she started kneading her clay again, just as if he wasn't there.'

'Oo, what a smart one she was!' remarked Aíchka.

'How so, my dear?'

'Whatever you please – she could answer him like that and he couldn't trip her up.'

'Oh no! He tripped her up all right, he really did!'

'How exactly?'

'He told her, "Can you be so deceived that you think you understand about God better than anyone else?"'

'She couldn't answer that and admitted, "I have a very

poor understanding of God and believe only in what I need to believe."

' "And what do you need to believe?"

' "That God exists, that it is His will that we should do good and not think our real life is here, but should prepare ourselves for eternity. And so, if I remember only that one thing, I then know at each moment what God requires of me, and what I must do. But when I begin to consider what each man should believe, where God is and what He is like – then I get all mixed up. Permit me not to go on with this conversation. You and I will never agree."

' "No, we won't agree," he said. "And I tell you, it is fortunate for you that you are living in this time of weakness; otherwise you might smolder on a stake."

' "Perhaps you would conduct me there?" she answered.

'She smiled herself, and he smiled and said to her affectionately, "Listen, my child: it grieves your mother so much that you are not settled, and it is the duty of children to pity their mothers."

'At that something seemed to snap in her and her eyes filled with tears.

' "Have mercy!" she said. "Do you really think that after living with my mother for twenty years I have less understanding and pity for her than you, who have come to us just now on her invitation?"

' "All right," he replied, "if you are such a good daughter, then choose yourself a worthy bridegroom."

' "I have already chosen him."

' "But your mother does not approve of this selection."

' "Mama doesn't want to find out what he is like."

' "What is there to find out, when he is an apostate?"

' "He is a Christian!"

' "Enough! Why should you not yield to your mother and select a husband from among your own people, people of circumstance and known to her and to your uncle?"

' "Why isn't the one I have chosen a man of circumstance?"

' "He is an apostate."

' "He is a Christian; he loves all men and does not distinguish among them by race and creed."

' "That is excellent. If he is indifferent, then have him adopt our faith."

' "What for?"

' "So that you may be bound together more closely."

' "We are already closely bound."

' "Then why not make it closer?"

' "Because nothing can unite us any closer than we are already united."

'He looked at her attentively and said, "And if you are mistaken?"

'Suddenly she answered sharply, "Excuse me, I am of age and I feel and understand what I am. I know what I was until a short time ago and what I have become now. I know that a new life has been born in me, and I will not exchange my present state for my former one. I love and respect my mother, but . . . You must know that 'He who is within us is greater than all' and I belong to Him and shall not give Him up to anyone, even to my mother."

'After saying that, she gasped for breath and blushed.

' "Excuse me," she said, "I seem to have answered you rudely, but I have nothing more to add." She moved the chair to get up.

'He also made a move and replied, "Well then, if you are so closely united . . . You feel a new life . . ."

'She stood up, looked at him severely and said, "Yes, we are united so closely that nothing can part us. It seems that we have nothing more to say!"

'He even swung away from her and said quietly, "It seems to me that you are slandering yourself."

'She answered him still more calmly, "No! Everything I have said is true."

'At that very moment Margaríta Mikháilovna gave a shriek and fell down in a faint on the floor. I, stupid sheep that I was, forgot I was standing on the edge of an ironing board and jumped down to help Margaríta. The ironing board flipped up and dropped Efrosínya Mikháilovna and smacked me below the belt with its other end. We all fell in a heap and lay there. The racket could be heard through the whole house. *He* heard it and stood up, saying to Klávdinka in great dismay, "What terrible disturbances! And all because of you!" She didn't say a word to that.

'Then he sighed and said, "Well, I cannot waste any more time. I am leaving."

'Klávdinka answered him quietly, "Good-bye."

' "Good-bye – and is that all? When you say good-bye to me, haven't you a single word to say from the heart?"

'At that, just imagine, she perked up and gave him both her hands. He was pleased and took her hands, saying, "Speak! Speak!"

'She answered him tenderly, "Take no notice of us; we have more of everything than we need. Go at once to those who are in want."

'With that she made him lose his temper. He seemed to choke when he replied, "I thank you, ma'am; I thank you!" and asked her not to show him out.'

12

'When he had made his appearance to the crowd outside the house, Klávdinka returned and came straight to the dark room where we were lying prostrate. She flung open the door and rushed to her mother. That Efrosínya and I were completely unable to get up – what did she care about that? Efrosínya Mikháilovna had dislocated her ninth rib, and I seemed to have broken my sacred Iliad. Besides that, we couldn't decide whether to be vexed or to laugh.

' "She's a fine girl!" I thought. "She told him everything . . . She herself doesn't hide . . ."

'So it all ended in this unheard-of and shameful disorder. We didn't see him get into his carriage: all the expectants were dispersed and again there was trickery and again he got into someone else's carriage and didn't notice, but started taking out letters. So they carried him off, and all our servants were terribly offended, because it had all come out differently from what they had expected. And then it turned out they had all heard Klávdinka herself, the mistress's daughter and heiress, beg him in front of everyone, "Take no notice of us!" What more did they need! I don't think he had ever heard that from anyone before. People had only begged and implored him with tears to make them happy, to come and visit them, but she seemed to chase him away: "Take no notice of us and go to those in want." There were angry discussions universally. The coachman Mirón, who had always been a boor – and besides he had drunk two more lickers – brought his duffers out into the courtyard to sprinkle them with holy water. His duffers had just been fed and were snorting, jumping around, and fighting. Mirón tried to pacify them by talking to them, but he wouldn't take them back to the stable for anything.

' "I," he said, "give glory to Thee, O Lord! I know formidably what the Law and Religion require: first of all the holy water is sprinkled on the masters and then in the same manner on the beasts."

'They took the horses away from him with some difficulty and took him off to bed, when suddenly Nikolái Ivánovich drove up in his most outstanding cups.'

'A vile man!' observed Aíchka.

'A real scoundrel!' confirmed Márya Martýnovna and went on: 'At that there was such an uproar that we were all completely worn out, and when twilight fell, everyone went to sleep on whatever couch he happened to be. But even in my sleep I dreamed how Klávdinka had distinguished herself with her shamelessness. Nikolái Ivánovich's snores could be heard through the whole house and Efrosínya was also sleeping face downward. But I couldn't even sleep – somebody seemed to be lifting me up, and it really was true. I pricked up my ears and heard that Margaríta Mikháilovna was not asleep either. She was walking around . . .

'I got so interested in this Margaríta of mine that I lay and made wheezing sounds as if I were asleep. But I had no mind to sleep; I kept the corner of my eye on her and listened to find out where she would go.

'She tiptoed through all the rooms, so quietly you could hardly hear her, and stopped by the jardinary. There she seemed to take some dry leaves in her hand; then she replaced the piece of sugar in the canary's cage, and picked up some little rag from the floor. She was listening herself, I noticed, to find out whether we were all sound asleep; then very quietly, tap-tap, she tiptoed out, like a thief.

'I sat right up on the couch and pricked up my ears. I heard her circling around through the hall and shuffling along toward Klávdinka's room. At that my heart gave a leap – what were they going to do?

'I rolled off the couch like a pea, tore off my slippers and put them under my arms, and running in my stocking feet made a different circle into the cloak room, from which there was a knot hole into Klávdinka's room over the door. Again I took my perch there very quietly, putting a chair on the table and standing on it. I looked in.

'It was half dark in the room. The lamp was burning, but the shade was pulled down so that the light came out only in one place, where she was modeling clay. She did that all herself – lit the lamp, put it out, and heated water in the samovar-top – all without the servants' help.

'And now, when the entire household was resting in peace, she, the zealous artisan, had already straightened up all her appurtenances as if nothing had happened.

'She was kneading and adding clay and modeling the devil knows what. I even looked at her figure to see whether there were any signs of what she had said about herself, but there was nothing yet, you couldn't see anything. She was still tall and slender.

'Her mother came in, but she didn't see her. My heart was pounding, thump-thump-thump. What would happen? Would the old woman give her a beating and would she take it submissively or, God have mercy, would she forget herself and raise her hand against her own mother? In that case I myself would be of use, because I would rush in and grab her arms and restrain her while her mother gave her a good lesson.'

13

'I held my breath. Margaríta Mikháilovna was standing in the semi-darkness and moving closer and closer to her . . .

'Then Miss Klávdinka gave a start and dropped her clay.

' "Mama dear!" she said. "You're not asleep! How you frightened me!"

'Margaríta restrained herself and said, "Since when has your mother become frightening to you?"

' "Why do you talk like that, Mama? You're not at all frightening to me. I am glad to see you, but I was busy and didn't hear anything . . . Sit down with me, Mama darling!"

'Suddenly Margaríta clasped her in both arms with her palms on her head and burst out, "Oh, Klávdinka, my own! My child, my little daughter, my treasure!"

' "Mama! What is the matter? Calm yourself."

'The old woman pressed her lips to Klávdinka's head; then suddenly she fell to her knees at Klávdinka's feet and wailed, "Forgive me, my angel! My sweet! I have offended you!"

' "This is a new twist!" I said to myself. I thought she had come to intimidate her with stern measures, and now she was asking her forgiveness.

'Klávdinka lifted her right up and put her in a chair and herself knelt in front of her and kissed her hands.

' "Mama darling," she said, "I don't remember anything you said to me in anger. You have always loved me, and I have been happy with you all my life; you have permitted me to study . . ."

' "Yes, yes, my darling, I was a fool. I let you study, and this is what has come of your studying!"

' "Nothing bad has come of it, Mama dear."

' "What do you mean, 'nothing'? What will people say about us now?"

' "What do you mean, Mama . . . ? Anyway, let them say what they please . . . People seldom say anything intelligent, Mama; much more often what they say is stupid."

' "That's just it: 'It's all stupid.' No, if it has already happened, then I consent, so as to hide your sin as soon as we can. Marry him; I consent."

'Klávdinka was amazed. "Mama! Darling! Are *you* saying that?"

' "Of course I am. Your happiness is dear to me; only don't leave my house – I would be lonely without you."

' "We will never leave you, Mama."

' "You won't leave me? He won't take you away from me?"

' "Not for anything, Mama!"

'The old woman clucked, "There, there! You've always been so good to me! And is he good?"

' "He is much better than I am, Mama."

' "Why is that?"

' "He is not afraid of death."

' "Well, why should he be? Let him live."

' "Do you feel for him?"

'Margaríta blinked and said through her tears, "Yes!"

'They embraced again and both of them burst out crying. Will you believe it, even I was touched!'

Aíchka agreed: 'Yes, it's very simple – they do touch you so!'

'Then Klávdinka calmly and without hurrying told her mother how his brother had had the kindest heart in the world and he did too: he would visit anyone, never quarreled with anyone, never asked anything for himself, forgave everyone everything, wasn't afraid of anyone, and didn't need anything.

' "Except you?"'

'She was embarrassed and replied, "Mama! I worship him so. He has taught me how to live . . . He has taught me to feel everything that hurts people . . . He has taught me to love people and their Father . . . and so I . . . I . . . shall be happy forever and ever!"'

' "Well, go ahead, go ahead. Only . . . why . . . did you let yourself go so far?"'

' "What do you mean, Mama?"'

' "Let's not talk about it. Only let's have your wedding as soon as possible, and then I'll feel at ease . . . I am willing to forgive you everything . . . It's only other people that turn me against you. My sister, and that tale-bearing woman Martýnikha."'

' "Forget her, Mama: don't be angry at her – she is unhappy."'

' "No, she is a vicious liar . . . She runs around everywhere and picks up gossip . . . I'll throw her out . . ."'

' "What are you saying, Mama! How can you throw anyone out? She is homeless. It would be better to give her some job so that she would have something to do and not to listen to the tales she bears about people. She doesn't understand how much harm she does."'

' "Yes she does understand; she and my sister kept after me saying that you were queer. They wore me down to the point where even I began to think you were queer. What can be done if I am as weak as that? . . . I believed them and sent her to invite *him*, and from this general expectension I got still more upset myself."'

' "It will all pass, Mama."'

' "Oh, no, my dear . . . What has happened to you . . . That won't pass."'

'Klávdinka looked at her perplexedly. "I don't understand you," she said.

' "Well, I'm not going to say anything if it's unpleasant for you. But I do think this: how can he be a seer if he can be tricked and put into someone else's carriage by treachery?"

' "Oh, let's not argue about that, Mama."

' "I was going to give him five hundred rubles, but now on account of the unpleasantness I'm going to send him a thousand tomorrow."

' "Send more, Mama. I am sorry for him."

' "Why should we be sorry for *him?*"

' "Of course we should, Mama . . . What a mission to take on oneself, what a part to play! People see him and lose their senses . . . They run around and crush one another like beasts and ask for money . . . Money!! Isn't it awful?"

' "Well, it's all the same to me . . . The bad thing is that now there will be gossip; and I don't like to have people saying bad things about you. But I do respect Nikolái Ivánovich, no matter what he is – hell-raiser and debachelor – because he quarrels with you face to face, but he won't let anyone say anything about you behind your back. 'For her,' he says, 'I'll give you a drubbing right now.' "

' "Uncle is a good man, and I am sorry for him – he is in darkness."

' "And why did they have to get up all this extraordinary business? All my life things have gone along in the ordinary way; our own priest would come and sing and have a bite to eat and play a game of cards and tell everyone 'God will forgive you.' "

' "In all cases, Mama, the simplest thing is the best."

' "Yes, he baptized you; let him marry you too. And let's not have Martýnikha here any more, so she won't play any more of her outstanding tricks."

'So that was all I would have got for all my troubles! But it was all decided differently, and quite unexpectedly.'

'Who decided it?' asked Aíchka.

'The cat, and I too a little bit,' continued Márya Martýnovna.

'But Klávdinka, to do her justice, finally stood up for me again and asked her mother to let me stay as a sort of out-standing servant in the house.

'The old woman replied, "All right, even though I don't want to, I'll let her stay for your sake."

'But my heart was all on fire. "Oh no," I thought. "I can get along without you. I'm no great shakes, but I have my pride, like the haughtiest beast of them all, and I have a lot of friends besides you in this town. I'll never go into service as a lady's maid."

'And I give you my word of honor that I meant to tiptoe right out of their house then and there, without saying good-bye to anyone, because heaven knows I am as proud as a beast. But imagine this: it didn't turn out that way.

'There was another incident that happened right on top of this one, and it held me back. While I was standing on the chair piled on top of the table, listening to their remarks, the fat cat got frisky, grabbed my felt slippers, which I had left on the floor, and the villain started knocking them all over the floor with his paw.

'Because of this trifle I was fairly gripped with terror. "The wretch," I thought, "will knock a slipper against some light chair or stool and make a noise, and they will come right in here and how will I look to them on my watchtower? How can I look at them and what will I think of to say about how I happened to be clambered up here on the table?"

'I climbed down, terribly afraid of falling, and began crawling around on the floor looking for my slippers. I crawled and crawled; I covered the whole floor, but I didn't find the slippers. Meanwhile I was awfully afraid that mother and daughter would have already made it up and would come out and see that I was not on the couch where I had been sleeping. And then how would I go back while they were there – and through Nikolái Ivánovich's rooms at that? What would they think? So I ran back without my slippers and got safely back to my place. Nikolái Ivánovich was sleeping with his collar off, not snoring or tossing. I lay back on the couch in my stocking feet and just had time to pretend to be asleep when Margaríta Mikháilovna and her daughter really did come in.'

14

'In a calm and collected voice Margaríta Mikháilovna ordered all the lamps to be lit and tea to be served, and she herself began waking everybody up for tea. When she came up to me, I said, "I'll get up myself right away." And I began looking for my slippers.

'And she, as if to spite me, asked, "What are you looking for?"

' "I am looking for my slippers."

' "Where did you put them?"

' "I had them on my feet."

' "Where could they have gone off your feet?"

' "I don't know myself."

' "Did your bridegroom come and take off your shoes? But that only happens at Christmas time."

' "No," I said. "I don't have any bridegrooms coming to me, but maybe it's a joke."

' "Tell me another! Who would want to make fun of you? Please, everyone look for Martýnovna's slippers."

'Where she got this irrepressible desire to look for my slippers – I don't yet understand. Just at that moment, to make matters worse, Nikolái Ivánovich came running out of his room in great excitement. He must not have had his sleep out or else he was frightened, because he was shouting, "Oo ay la damn? Oo ay la damn?"

'His sisters-in-law answered him "What are you saying, sir? What are you saying? Damn . . . ?"

'He was actually shaking with fury and replied, "Damn means woman!"

'Margaríta Mikháilovna made the sign of the cross over him and said, "What woman?"

' "The one who has just done something vile to me."

' "What did she do? What was vile? Can't you tell us?"

'He tossed his head like a goat and in the most imperative mood said, "I'll put this item on the gender for all of you: What bitch woke me up and left this slipper of hers on my bed?"

'And he showed them my slipper in his hand. Well, naturally, everyone thought it was funny.

'But I replied, "That slipper is mine, but we must find out how it got there."

'But he didn't listen to me. "Everyone knows," he said, "how such things get there."

'At that point the boy Egórka, the stove-tender, rushed in all pale and shouted, "Someone is throwing something around behind the stove in our bathroom!"

'We went there, and there in the bathtub was my other slipper swimming around in the water, and that accursed cat was sitting on the edge of the stove.

' "Good Lord!" I exclaimed. "What is this? If everyone is trying to drive me out, I had better go myself."

'And Nikolái Ivánovich hurried me on. "Do us a favor, get out! We'll get along better without you!" And with that he turned my face to the mirror and said, "Take a look at yourself and put this item on the gender: is it decent for you to go playing with your slippers?"

'The devil only knows what he meant by that in his drunken state of forgetfulness, and those foolish women told me they had drawn the interjection that I had been in his room and had followed him everywhere, even into the bathroom.'

'And maybe you really did?' drawled Aíchka.

'Enough of that, please! As if I could fix it so that one foot was in his room and the other in the bathroom! It is unthinkable to tear yourself apart like that! But just imagine, that stupid old woman got offended and began whispering, "I don't condemn anyone," she said. "But why should this happen just in my house, and just after a visitation . . ."

'I couldn't hold back and in return plunged a good fencing thrust into her chest: "Don't say any more, please," I said, "about this being your house and just after a visitation! . . . Some people did such a job of showing the visitor out that they practically kicked him out." And I told her how Klávdia had begged him to take no notice of everyone in the house and hurry off to people in want.

'But Nikolái Ivánovich thought that was as it should be. "So he should," he said. "What was he doing here anyway? He ought to go off to the farms where the crops have failed and pray them in a big harvest for the multiplication of the loaves. He ought really to be ashamed of hanging around well-fed people like us."

' "Why do you keep talking about shameful things to me?" I replied. "It's not me that does the shameful things in your house . . . Look for it a little closer home . . ."

'As always, Nikolái Ivánovich liked to vent his malice on whoever came to hand, and he rushed at me like a hawk at a chicken and began to strangle me.'

'Oh, my God!' said Aíchka sympathetically.

'Yes, yes, yes,' Márya Martýnovna went on. 'His sisters-in-law couldn't even get me away from him. He would have choked me to death, but Klávdia came in and said, "Uncle, let go!" just like she was shouting at a poodle. So he let me go. Then Margaríta took five hundred rubles out of her bedroom and said to me, "Here, Márya Martýnovna, are five hundred rubles as a reward from me to you. Now do as you please: either take this money for what you have suffered, or make a complaint against Nikolái Ivánovich and may God be with you. I am not angry with you, and if you would like to say good-bye to us nicely, I will give you still more, but please go."

' "I don't make any complaint," I said, "because I am Orthodox."

'But Nikolái Ivánovich bellowed, "It's not because of that. You know that if you make a complaint, you'll get less."

' "You can suppose what you please," I said. "But I don't want them to pronounce in court the sacred name of personality along with the maidenly secrets of Miss Klávdia."

'At that he would have broken loose again, but Klávdia grabbed him and took him away and went out herself. Margaríta gave me three hundred rubles more and said, "Dear friend, here, take this for yourself and go away. There's no use waiting here any more."

' "I'm not going to wait," I said.'

'And you took the money?' asked Aíchka.

'You don't think I'd leave it to them!'

'Right! Or else Klávdinka would sneak off to her "friends in need"!'

'Naturally!'

They were silent.

'Is that what you call saying good-bye "nicely"?' asked Aíchka.

'Yes, I packed my things and by mistake instead of "Good night" I told them "May God rest your souls!" and went off.'

'And you're not sorry that it turned out like that?'

'I'm not sorry; it's a sin to be sorry: they brought it all on themselves. God imperatively visited their sins upon them to make up for the way they behaved at the visit of His holy messenger. Their household had been outstanding in its magnificence, but now one calamitry has followed another and they have been reduced to the most ordinary position. And it all came from Klávdia Rodiónovna's tactical education, and if nobody puts a stop to it, she'll mix everybody up in her dilutions.'

'Do you mean everybody started modeling appurtenances?' asked Aíchka.

'No, she did the modeling, and now they even give her orders for statutes, but she has brought still worse consequences on the members of her family.'

'For instance, what has happened to them?'

'Well, for instance, this is what has happened: to begin with Nikolái Iványch. Once when he was coming back from his musket-earing he forgot what he had forgotten.'

'My!'

'And it turned out later that he had forgotten he had in his pocket a dispatch from his son Petrúsha saying that he was returning the next day from his trip around the world. He did return and came one morning in a cab when no one expected him, and only then did his father remember the dispatch. He gave his son the worst possible reception and almost wouldn't even see him.

'"I have no need of any trans-Atlantic idiot," he said.

'But Klávdia was nice to this Petrúsha and only threatened

her uncle with one finger of her left hand. Then she took charge of Pétinka and got him to the point where, though homeless himself, he asked his father's permission to marry that same niece of Krutílda, on whose account his father had exiled him. His father naturally wouldn't hear of it, and anyway it was unthinkable to allow it, because in the meantime she had committed still another transgression. None of us knew anything about it, but Klávdia Rodiónovna did, because it turned out that she had traced that individual, tracked her down in her misery, and had been supporting her at the old woman's place where I had followed her. There she had shielded her from all misfortunes and visited her, and finally convinced her cousin with this argument: "You are to blame for her fall, since it was because you abandoned her that she fell again. You must smooth it over and take her and never reproach her with anything, because you yourself are responsible for all her misfortunes." And she read the Gospel to him again to the effect that he daren't marry any other woman but that one and finally she won him over – Pétya agreed. Then she came and begged her uncle to let them marry and tried to convince him that the girl had a very kind heart and that her transgression resulted only from her being abandoned.

'The old man said, "I suppose the item on the gender is: you think it's a good thing?"

' "It is not good," replied Klávdia, "but it is the sort of thing you must forgive, because it all came about on account of you. He who abandons a helpless woman is himself responsible for her downfall."

' "Where is that written?"

'She was about to reach for her Gospel, but he took her hand. "Let it go," he said.

' "No, I won't let it go, and if you are going to be cruel and demand that he abandon her for the second time, then it will be still worse for her."

' "How will it be worse?" he asked.

' "You know better than I," she said, "what awaits those whom you lure away from the path of righteousness and then abandon. But you should know this: your son is no longer in your power."

' "Whose power is he in?"

' "In the power of Him with Whom you will not dare to dispute: Pétya will hearken not to you, but to Him. The temptations of the world are not from Him."

' "So you are stirring him up against me?"

' "No, I am not," said Klávdia, "but I say that they must not abandon each other! It leads to suffering and sin. After that Pétya would never be able to live with a clear conscience. I have convinced him and I shall continue to urge him to respect the will of his Heavenly Father more than that of his earthly father. And if you will not listen to what I tell you about eternal life, you will die an eternal death."

'She talked and talked and browbeat him and wore him down until he was like a fish on a hook: his mouth was open and he didn't know what to say.

'And then Petrúsha started repeating the same thing after her, that his conscience had tormented him for three years in all sorts of places and still wouldn't give him any peace and that he had taken the guilt of this erring girl upon his own conscience and wanted to amend her life and his own.

'At that Nikolái Ivánovich began biting his lips and suddenly said, "I suppose we must die and we really are all sinners. You look at a young mam'selle and right away you start thinking of ways to fix her so that the next day she won't be Mam'selle any more, but Gut Morgen. That is the viciousness of our whole sinphony; but Klávdia walks straight ahead!"

'And he gave his son his blessing to get married before the law and suddenly he even grew very fond of their little boy, his grandson, and even began introducing them to everyone, "This is my son, Mr Europe, and this is my grandson, Master Asia Minor."

'But Krutílda had kept her pride and wouldn't stand for that. She went and married her Alconse and turned over Nikolái Ivánovich's IOUs so that he would be put in debtor's prison.'

'She got him in a nice mess,' remarked Aíchka, laughing.

'Yes. But Klávdinka wouldn't let her uncle go to prison; she begged a mint of money from her mother. "This will be my dowry," she said. And so her mother paid for him, and they sold their house and began living the whole year round at the factory. They are still living the year round in that hole, and Klávdinka likes it very much.'

'And I suppose her beauty is fading there?' asked Aíchka.

'Naturally, everything is fading with that fool, but in spite of that the wretch is still very good-looking.'

'And what about her Versteht?'

'With him things took a still purer turn.'

'Did she marry him or not?'

'She didn't marry anybody!'

'He ducked out of it?'

'No, he didn't duck out, but they both started surpassing each other in one thing after another, and finally she packed him off to the next world.'

'In what manner?'

'None!'

'But what happened then?'

'Nothing happened. "We have found," she said, "that we don't need to take any obligations on ourselves and we also don't need to have a family." They decided to remain friends according to their faith and that was all.'

'What monsters!'

'Lunatics!'

'But how did she kill him off?'

'No one knew anything about it. Suddenly she came home very pale and didn't tell anyone anything, and later it turned out that he had died.'

'Just like that!'

'Yes. Some poor child had gotten such an infection in its throat that no one would treat it at home. Following his brother's example, he went and for the sake of others wrote down everything about the disease, but he himself caught the infection and died.'

'Was she very broken up?'

'I don't know how to say it – it was like she had turned to stone. Her mother said, "Well, everyone knows about your sin; if you were not ashamed before God, it is not worth being ashamed before men. Go and say good-bye to him and kiss him in his coffin. You will feel better." But she only burst into sobs and fell on her mother's shoulders, saying, "Mama darling! I have already said good-bye to him."'

'Did she confess?'

'Yes. "When he started going there," she said, "I kissed him while he was alive; forgive me for that."'

'You mean that was all there was to it, that she had kissed him once?'

'So she said.'

'But what about . . . what she had confessed to before?'

'What was that?'

'Well, all you told me about . . .'

'Oh, about her conjugation in an indefinitive state?'

'Yes.'

'Well, that remained in an indefinitive state.'

'How did it come out?'

'Just that, nothing came out at all.'

'You mean you had made up a pack of lies about her then?'

'I don't mean that at all; I mean only that I expected what would have followed according to the consummation of all the probabilities, but with them everything is turned around. It turned out that the "new life" she had found in herself had been nothing but divine, as though Christ had united them only in their eternal thoughts. Just think how she could dare to think that up and claim such sanctity for herself!'

It took Aíchka some time to squeeze out an answer. 'No, that's nothing. But where did they get the patience to live like that!'

'It's awful! Awful! There was absolutely no way you could upset them . . . No matter what you did to aggravate and insult them, they took it all, as if earthly grief didn't concern them in the least!'

'I think people didn't know how to pester them properly.'

'Maybe so.'

'No, definitely.'

'What would you have done to them?'

'I'd put them barefoot on a hot frying pan and let them sizzle a bit.'

'That's the way! That's the way! But they say that's cruelty.'

Aíchka did not reply. She had either gone to sleep or perhaps had begun thinking of something 'off the subject'.

15

Márya Martýnovna stood up, went off somewhere, and then sat down in her place again. During that time Aíchka gave a sigh and said, without any apparent bearing on anything, 'Sterile word-mongers!'

Márya Martýnovna understood what she meant and caught up her remark. 'Yes, that's right! Some other girl might have a simple heart and live her life and do everything on the quiet and go to confession and repent of everything quietly. And no one would know anything. But these fools – wherever they step, they knock things about and then deprive them-selves of any happiness. Later they shorten their lives by living for others, while they themselves remain in an indefinitive state . . . No, you just put this item on the gender for me: what's to be done with them to get them out of it?'

But Aíchka was silent again, and Márya Martýnovna resumed the conversation herself.

'Well, let's take your word for it, that people don't know what to do to them; I'll agree with you. But why are they so peculiar that they don't have any tears, never plead with anyone or complain, but accept everything that is done to them as if it had to be like that?'

'They are pretending.'

'That's just what I think! For heaven's sake tell me this: such a disaster had just taken place – her fiancé had died. But the very day she buried him she sat down to work and even started a school to teach poor children for nothing. How did she get that way? But there's one good thing about it. Even though you say people don't know what to do with them, still they don't let them start up any little thing they please: her school was soon closed. But note this: again this time she wasn't at all bothered and didn't complain.'

'They are incorrigible.'

'That's just it! What can you do with them when they are so free from sorrow? They closed her school, but now she does services for everyone in whatever ways she can. She gives out books to children and sits down with them to read wherever she happens to be.'

'That shouldn't be allowed either.'

'There was a prohibition; on account of the books the district police officer came to make a general investigation of all her books. But when he looked through them, he left them all with her and even started apologizing.

' "I have carried out my orders," he said, "and I am ashamed of myself." '

'That's a good one for you!'

'That's not all! When she told him she was not offended and held out her hand to him, he even kissed her hand and said, "Forgive me; you are a righteous woman." '

'I suppose she won't get married now?'

'Her mother asked her whether she had taken a vow after the death of her first sweetheart not to marry anyone else. She replied that she didn't take vows. According to them it's not proper to take vows either. The old woman kept asking whether she hadn't perhaps promised the departed not to marry anyone. She said no to that too.

' "Then perhaps you will gladden my heart and get married?"

'But she gave the same answer to that. "I don't know, Mama, but I don't think so."

' "Why not?"

' "It's very hard to live with me, Mama."

'She admitted herself that it was hell living with her. And then on her mother's name-day she gave her mother a fine present by saying, "Mama darling! I am yours! On this day, your name-day, I have made up my mind and have given myself up to serving you and the poor. I shall not marry."

'That's the way things were left, and she is still living as an old maid. Instead of bearing her own children and surrounding them with love and tenderness and passing on to them the remnant of her capital, she has again collected a lot of ragged children and gives them clothes and sings to them about the frog on the path.'

16

The conversation stopped. Márya Martýnovna was probably enjoying the pleasure of having brought her narrative to a conclusion in which her principal enemy, Klávdinka, had been put to shame. Aíchka made no response, perhaps because her mind was far away, thinking of something.

This conjecture was confirmed. After a rather prolonged interval she sighed and said, 'Anyway, it really surprises me!'

'What's that?'

'Just imagine, I know an idiot just like that too.'

'A man?'

'Yes, and a very interesting one, but this same foolishness has got hold of him too.'

'Tell me, what kind of monstrosities does he commit?'

'Just like that girl: there's nothing he wants – good things to eat, nice clothes to wear – nothing in the world.'

'And he doesn't need a woman's love either?'

'Imagine – he doesn't.'

'That can never be! No matter what the situation, that doesn't go out of fashion.'

'Oh yes, that's just it – it is going out!'

'I won't believe it for anything!'

'How can you help believing it, when I assure you it's true?'

'I just don't believe it, my dear one. A man can always be tempted by a woman's figure.'

'And I am telling you, my cheap one, that he won't be tempted.'

Márya Martýnovna seemed to choke on something, but she recovered herself and said, 'Of course, my day is past.'

'Even if your day weren't past, and even if you didn't have a needle inside you, you still couldn't convince me.'

'Why is that?'

'Because they are completely inhuman. They don't worship beauty at all, but look for somebody who agrees with their ideas. So if you happen to fall in love with one of them, you get nothing but displeasure out of it.'

'Do you like him very much?'

'How did you know?'

'Isn't it obvious? You ruin everything by showing your feelings to him like that.'

'I'm not ruining anything; I just disgust him.'

'The way a coin disgusts a beggar?'

'No, I disgust him completely.'

'How can a rich young girl like you disgust anybody? What an outstanding idiot he must be!'

'He's not an idiot, but he's the same sort as that Klávdinka of yours. He keeps looking up things in the Gospel and trying to live simply and work and think about the poor – that's the sort of empty pleasure he gets out of life.'

'Can't you attract him with all your capital?'

'Oh, what does he want with capital, when he doesn't need anything more than he has! You give him something nice to eat, and he answers, "I don't need it; I've already had enough." You ask him to drink your health and he says, "Why should I drink? I'm not thirsty." '

'Really, what kind of monster is that!'

'Yes; I won't live like that for anything.'

'Naturally. Let him pick himself a wife that suits their style.'

But when she heard that, Aíchka shrieked, 'Wha-a-at?' and added sharply that she would never permit that.

'I'd rather see him on the table under a shroud than with another woman!'

'Well, that's a possibility,' Martýnikha soothed her in a tranquil tone.

Aíchka lowered her voice. 'That is – what? Can you really do that?'

'Put him under a shroud?'

'Yes . . . After all, a person might have to answer for that.'

'You only have to wash out his shirt for him and put it on him for the night . . . That's all.'

'Oo, what a vicious one you are!'

'But it's for your sake I would do it!' Martýnikha cut her off in some confusion.

'No, how could you dare to think of that for my sake! To wash out a shirt!'

'Well, let it drop, please. I suppose you can see I was joking!'

'You were joking! No, you thought you had found a foolish girl in love, and I would give you such a commission, and then I'd be in your power. I'm no fool!'

'And who told you you were a fool, my dear one!'

'That's just it, my cheap one!'

'O, Lord save us!'

'Yes, yes, yes.'

'But how would you like to live?'

'To have him be my husband and live the way I want him to. That's all.'

'Then maybe it would be better to explain it to him straight off: "I love you; let's get married." '

'There, can you imagine it? I have already been brought to that level of baseness. I did explain it to him.'

'What did he do – get on his high horse?'

'Not in the least. He only pressed my hand and said, "Raísa Ignátyevna, you are mistaken on that score." I even had a fit of hysterical weeping and I said, "No, I love you and I'll give you all my capital." But he . . .'

Aíchka suddenly burst into tears and sobbed and sobbed.

'There, there, my sweet, don't make yourself miserable,' Márya Martýnovna begged her.

'Don't stroke me, I don't like it!' Aíchka said capriciously.

'Well, all right, all right, I won't. What did he say to you?'

'He didn't believe me, the fool.'

Again tears were audible.

'Well, in that case he lacks either feelings or understanding,' Márya Martýnovna decided.

'No, he has feelings, and he really understands very well. But he said, "You are mistaken in your feelings – it is my despicable flesh that you love and you want to herd swine with me, but you don't love me for myself, and you can't love me in that way, because you and I disagree in our ideas and we work for different masters. I want to work for my own master and I don't want to herd swine with you." '

'What's that? . . . What's that for? . . . What did he mean

about herding swine and working for different masters?' drawled Márya Martýnovna in perplexity.

'That's just the point! If you don't understand, then don't argue with me!' replied Aíchka in a tremulous voice. A moment later she added still more angrily, 'According to them consoling yourself with love is called "herding swine".'

'Ugh!'

Márya Martýnovna gave a loud spit of disgust and cried, 'Swine! I swear, they are swine themselves!'

'Yes,' replied Aíchka. 'He said worse things than that . . . He'll pay for it . . .'

'For what, sweet, for what? What else did he . . . How did he insult you?'

'He insulted me terribly . . . He said I was not a Christian, that a Christian couldn't live with me and bring up children to be Christians . . . !'

'Ugh, he'll pay for that!'

'Yes, I told him that. "I fast and take Communion," I said, "and you never do . . . Which one of us is a Christian?"'

'He'll pay.'

'I can't change my character!'

'Don't try! Why should you spoil them!'

'I told him I would get embittered and that if I pleased, I would give away all my money, but I would do it the way I wanted and not their way.'

'Well, now I understand you . . . why you came here! Of course, they'll carry you in their arms here!'

'A lot of use I have for that! But you don't understand anything at all!'

'No, now you've let it out.'

'I didn't let it out the least bit. I'm simply going to test

whether it is true that by praying here you can make someone's heart ache and fix everything the way you want it.'

But Márya Martýnovna interrupted her at that. 'My angel!'
she exclaimed heatedly. 'Here you can arrange everything by
prayer. This place is just like Mount Tabor. But you should
know that God won't answer prayers for evil.'

Aíchka lost her temper completely. 'What sort of nonsense
are you talking!' she shrieked. 'What do you mean by "prayers
for evil", when all I want to do is to lead him out of homeless
loneliness into lawful matrimony and then fix it so that he will
finally like the things everybody else likes?'

'Yes. That is, that he would not cleave unto the simple life,
but should seek for himself not only what is of benefit to the
soul, but also what is of benefit to the body?'

'That's all!'

'Yes, if that is all, then of course that is the blessed law of
matrimony, and in that case God will certainly aid you.'

'Yes, and now you please keep quiet, because it will soon
be dawn and I am very upset and will look pale.'

The Scheherazade was over. My neighbors said nothing
more; perhaps they had gone to sleep. Following their sens-
ible example, I too went into a brief doze just before morning.
But I awoke soon after, left some money on the table to pay for
my 'expectension', and departed from Rome without seeing
the Pope.

The trip had been of benefit to me after all; I felt more
cheerful. It was as if I had grown rich on impressions. And
now, whenever I happen to be returning late at night through
streets where merchants live and see the multicolored icon
lamps glowing in their houses, I no longer imagine there
merely shameless hypocrites or the timid and hopeless

snivelers of the 'dark kingdom'. I feel there the invigorating spirit of Klávdinka breathing upon me, a spirit providing resources for life in any situation in which the will of the Most High sees fit to perfect in the struggle against darkness that which is born of light.